MONICA LA PORTA

THE PRIEST

BOOK ONE OF THE GINECEAN CHRONICLES

To my husband, Roberto. Always.

TABLE OF CONTENTS

CHAPTER 1

Mauricio had not slept well; he played with the collar rubbing against the skin on his neck. He had shared his small cell with three other men for the last week. It wasn't the first time, but his body was bigger now and he occupied more space. The muscles in his legs were aching. He needed to stretch them, but there was no space to walk between his bed, a narrow plank of wood, and the wall. Three snoring bodies were fighting for comfort on the dirty floor.

He raised his arms over his head and stretched his neck. He flattened his back against the wall and then pressed down to hug his legs. "How can this be so painful?" he asked himself. His calves were in knots. *Not a cramp.* It was his left foot. *Not again,* he thought and then swore out loud.

"Stop making so much noise; it's impossible to sleep," one of the men complained.

Yeah right, because you were resting so comfortably before I spoke out loud. Mauricio almost laughed. Almost. Then his right foot cramped too, and he didn't think it was funny anymore.

"Silence!" the guard outside his cell ordered. She had a screeching voice.

I'd give anything to shut your mouth once and for all. "And if I don't? What?" Mauricio knew better than to antagonize the guard, a woman who held his future in her bony hands. But he couldn't help himself.

"Get out." The guard opened the cell door and pointed her gun at him.

Mauricio noticed that she had a whip ready in her other hand. "Right away," he murmured under his breath.

His legs weren't steady enough and the hesitation in his movements earned Mauricio a taste of the guard's spitefulness. He

1

managed to suppress a scream when the whip lashed his chest, but a tear escaped his eye. *I hate you with all my heart.* He turned his head to hide his pain from the guard. The three men remaining in the cell were silently fighting for the empty bed. To Mauricio the sight was more painful than the whiplash. He was aware of his condition as a slave. Sometimes he wondered if the other men were.

"You worthless excuse for a slave should thank the Heavens the Priestess seems to think you could be of some use in the Temple. If it were up to me, I would have put you out of your misery already," the guard said.

Mauricio didn't utter another word. He walked through the dimly lit hallway with the point of the whip pressed firmly against his shoulder blade. His legs straightened with each step he took on the hay-covered dirt floor. *At least I'm outside my cell; maybe I'll get some sleep after all,* Mauricio thought, satisfied by the turn of events. The feeling didn't last long.

"Here, spend the rest of the night in better company." The guard pushed Mauricio inside a dark cell that smelled of rotten fish. She laughed loudly at her joke while she closed the door of the isolation chamber.

"Thanks," he said, grinning. He could have done without another set of fresh bruises. Still, defying women was one of the pleasures of his young life.

He sat on the crude floor, letting his eyes adjust to the darkness. He knew the place all too well. Normally after a few days of total isolation, he could make out shapes. The prolonged starvation produced images to keep his brain occupied while his stomach was painfully empty. He smiled. He could sleep undisturbed now.

"Wake up. You're wanted elsewhere." The guard's voice echoed inside his cell.

Today we have brutality with a side of loud banging against the door, he thought, his eyes still closed despite all the noise.

The woman barged in, the stomping of her reinforced boots waking him completely. *Nothing says 'good morning' like the fear of being beaten.* He directed his thoughts toward a happier place.

This kind of mental reasoning was his lifeline. He occupied himself for hours with this endeavor. Right now, it helped him to look ahead and filter out the barrage of insults bestowed upon him. It was a wonder he hadn't gone mad. The guards weren't smart or creative. After eighteen years, he had heard all the possible variations of how worthless he was. There weren't too many of them.

"Idiot, listen to me." A crack of the whip on the floor accompanied the order.

The crack against the floor and not his skin made Mauricio suddenly aware. *Why haven't you given me my morning whipping yet?* It was a first. Firsts of any kind made him wary.

"Behave yourself," the guard said with another crack of the whip. She aimed closer, but refrained from hitting him.

Mauricio followed the woman through a long hallway he had never seen before. It had a high-vaulted ceiling supported by brick walls. Mauricio noticed the bricks because the hallway was lit by a myriad of sconces. He walked along with growing fear. He had heard stories. Young men disappeared from their cells and never came back. Nobody knew what happened to them.

"Stay put and wait your turn." The woman left him.

The white room was barren of both humans and furnishings. The light was too intense for Mauricio's unaccustomed eyes. He shielded his eyes with an outstretched hand, but the white glare seeped through his slim fingers. A new smell assaulted his nose. It was crisp and cold, leaving a citrus aftertaste on his palate.

"You, come here," a voice called; then a woman's head emerged from a door he hadn't seen. He realized that there were several white doors concealed in the walls.

"Hurry up." She was getting annoyed.

Mauricio moved right away. In his experience with women in general, he discovered it was wise to jump to orders immediately. He went through the door and into another white room. This one was warmer and more humid than the former, a pleasant surprise—Mauricio was always cold.

"Remove your clothes, shower, and don this gown," the voice commanded.

Mauricio looked around and discovered that he was in a room covered from floor to ceiling with white tiles. *Blasted tiles*, he thought, sliding in his worn slippers despite his attempt to control himself. He stripped to his underwear and moved to one of the shower stalls lining the wall in front of him.

"Remove everything. When you're done, you'll have a new set of clothes," the woman said in a bored voice. Mauricio reluctantly tossed his underwear on the bench by the pile of clothing. Although he didn't possess anything, not even those clothes, he had been wearing the ragged garments for some time now and had formed an attachment to them. He thought of them as *his*.

"Scrub your skin with the soap." The woman didn't look at him; she was giving instructions while dialing numbers on her cell phone.

Mauricio did as ordered. *This isn't bad.* The water was hot and the soap had the same citrus scent he had smelled in the other room. He turned toward the wall to gain some privacy. The idea was silly, he knew that, but it made him feel better as he washed his private parts. Mauricio enjoyed a few more minutes of unspoiled happiness. He closed his eyes and opened his senses to the experience.

"Don the gown." The woman's voice intruded on his moment of peace.

Mauricio reluctantly turned off the water and hastily dried his body with a small towel lying on the short wall separating his shower stall from the next. The towel was already wet; someone had used it before him. His body barely dry, he reached for the green gown hanging from a hook and finished drying his skin with the rough fabric.

"You are done here. Go to the next room." The woman opened a door next to her and rushed him away without interrupting her phone call.

Mauricio went from the steamy warmth of the room where he showered to the freezing cold of an icy-blue chamber. He couldn't fathom what this room's function was. The door closed behind him and he was left to stare at the activity before his eyes. He wasn't the only slave in the room. There were several young men,

4

probably around his age; some he recognized from the working room. All of them were wearing the same green gown. They were also standing in a line, waiting their turn to be inspected by an older woman with white hair sitting at the end of the room.

From his corner, Mauricio couldn't see what the older woman was doing to them. They weren't screaming, though, which was reassuring. He stepped behind the last man in line.

"What is she doing?" Mauricio whispered to the man in front of him.

"I don't know," answered the man, whose voice revealed he was nothing but a scared boy.

Mauricio thought it wiser to wait for his turn and not say anything else. He did as the others did. Finally, he was in front of the older woman. She opened his mouth, looked at his teeth, muttered something unintelligible, and scribbled a few notes on a pad sitting on her lap. She patted his legs with uninterested hands and wrote another note. Then she yanked open his gown and gave him a brief look. Several notes followed. When Mauricio thought he was through with the procedure, she groped his genitals with two cold fingers. *What are you doing?* With wild eyes, he recoiled at her probing.

"Fill this and take it to the last room at the end of the hall." The older woman gestured toward a tray with transparent plastic cups. Mauricio picked up the cup and left.

CHAPTER 2

Mauricio looked down, satisfied he hadn't spilled anything on the floor. He put the specimen cup on the tray and waited for the window to open. He then sat on the only chair in the small, aseptic place, mindlessly fidgeting with his collar; it only tickled if he gently tugged at it, but it stung if he tried to walk through the outer doors. Mauricio had foolishly tried enough to know. There were scars hidden behind the rigid, metal cuff attesting to that. Nevertheless, four years after being *chosen* to be a semental, he still longed to be outside.

He had given his quota for the day and now he only had to wait patiently to be brought back to his cell. It didn't make him feel good. He felt guilty every time the field crew came back from a long day of laboring outside in the desert heat. He was living an easier life compared to theirs, a privilege he resented. The other men despised those like him. They came back from the fields with bruises and wounds. He stayed in the Temple, ate three warm meals daily and stayed in his own cell where he could rest during the day. His face was unmarred by hideous scars, and even those on his body had almost faded. The women kept him fit. He had to exercise every day and had regular physiological checkups. But he didn't have friends. And he was never allowed outside.

Mauricio knew that this *privileged* life wasn't going to last forever. Sooner or later he would have to share the harshness of the sun on his back with the field crews. He was looking forward to it. He wanted to belong. More than anything else, he wanted to be able to stand up and look the other men in the eye without feeling ashamed. And he wanted freedom. But that was the dream of every man in Ginecea. Mauricio was a slave. His father had been a slave. His father's father had been a slave. His entire paternal lineage had probably never tasted freedom.

Mauricio had never met his mother. He knew she was a fathered woman, a lesser citizen who didn't belong to the pure breed race. For the greater good of Ginecea, her purpose in life was to bear future slaves to serve the pure breeds. Fathered women weren't kept in captivity like the men, but they had a limited freedom and couldn't own property. Sometimes Mauricio thought about the woman who had conceived him—maybe she wasn't evil. He couldn't imagine her being like the pure breed guards who had treated him like scum since the day he was born. Pure breeds never gave birth to men. Never. They only conceive women.

Mauricio was curious about that. There were rumors among the other men. Nobody bothered to talk directly to him, but Mauricio heard them talking at night. Some of the men knew things. Exactly how they knew the things they knew wasn't clear.

There was an older man in particular whom everyone called Sapiente. He liked to spin tales at night. He loved to talk and the other men enjoyed listening to his voice. He shared several theories regarding the way the pure breeds' precious little girls came to be. One theory had always fascinated Mauricio.

"The Priestess is the only one who knows how to make pure breed baby girls. She has some women helping her called Ancillae. Pure breed couples from all over Ginecea come to the Temple to become pregnant. They decide what characteristics they want in the baby and then wait for the Priestess to add the soul, which is called the incognito." Sapiente, who had supposedly served the fathered women who worked in a separate area inside the Temple, used to repeat this story almost every night, managing to keep the facts consistent, which by itself was noteworthy.

Thinking on all of this, he couldn't sympathize with his biological mother. Her life was a thousand times better than what fate had dealt his father. He had lived with him until he was six years old and was then placed in a communal living quarter with other boys. He could still hear the little kids cry at night, looking for their dads to come back. He had missed his father terribly and dreamed of him often. But he couldn't remember the shape of his eyes or the color of his hair. His dad's soft voice was the only thing he could recall. Mauricio could still hear his dad singing lullabies at night to help him sleep before the guards could complain about his crying. His voice had a warm tone that wrapped Mauricio's little body like a blanket.

A knock on the wall. "Hey, are you still there?" Someone was speaking to him. He was probably another semental, waiting for the guards.

"Yes." Mauricio never knew what to say when someone tried to start a conversation with him. He wasn't used to exchanging friendly words anymore.

"Something is wrong," the other man commented, and Mauricio realized that he had been waiting much longer than usual.

"Why do you think that is?" Mauricio hesitantly asked.

"I heard the guards complaining about a pure breed," the man said, lowering his voice for fear of being heard.

"Really?" Mauricio found that piece of information difficult to believe. Pure breeds were a loyal race.

"The guards were outside my room and they called the girl 'the Presidential brat,'" the man said in an even lower whisper.

"And why were they complaining about her?" Mauricio asked. He liked the idea of spending some time chatting with the man.

"They said that *the brat* is forcing them to work double time. And they don't like it," the man finished.

"Interesting," Mauricio conceded, but truthfully, he didn't believe a single word the man had said, nor did he care about their captors' *miserable* lives. *Pure breeds could all die, and Ginecea would be a better place, if you ask me.* Still, he was having a meaningful exchange with another human being.

"There will be repercussions," the man said, his voice shaking.

"Of that I am sure."

A sudden thump announced the end of their brief camaraderie. The door opened and a guard faced Mauricio with an expression that didn't bode well; his heart sunk. The man was telling the truth and Mauricio was going to pay for whatever was annoying the guards.

"You… produce some more." The guard placed another cup on the tray, carefully avoiding touching him, even by mistake. Pure breeds only interacted with men by ordering them around, and when the voice commands weren't enough, they beat them. They never touched slaves. Pure breeds were repulsed by men.

"But I have just—" It wasn't the first time some clumsy guard lost a tray with the specimen, and he couldn't help but complain. A mistake he hadn't made in a while.

"How dare you? Do what I say, and do it fast," the guard threatened while showing him the whip.

He knew the guards were under orders not to physically abuse the sementals, but he also knew accidents had happened in the past. He lowered his head and retrieved the cup. The guard closed the door behind her with an insult Mauricio didn't understand; she had a thick northern accent. He had already given his quota and had no energy to produce more, and yet he had no choice.

Guards had subtle ways to punish sementals when they didn't comply with orders. The privilege of better meals and extra water were strategically paraded about to provoke the other slaves' anger, achieving their desired result: a good beating executed by the men.

Mauricio put the cup on the tray and waited. Again. The tray hadn't disappeared behind the window as it normally would, although the guard had already returned.

"Follow me," the usual order came at him.

Mauricio was surprised when the guard didn't return him to his cell. Instead, he was locked in another room.

"Prepare yourself in case we need more." The guard gave him a cold look and left him alone in the new room.

Mauricio sat on the floor thinking about the inane order. *Prepare myself, again? How?* He would have laughed, but a strong headache was looming. He simply bent his legs and rested his face on his lap, hoping that the pain he was feeling on his left temple would disappear.

"Is the table ready?" A woman's voice echoed in his room. "Are the instruments sterilized already?" the same voice asked, after another woman had affirmed the first question. They kept talking about other things, but their voices were lower now, almost an indistinct buzz.

Mauricio looked around the room to see where their voices were coming from. After a few seconds, he found a ventilation grid and listened intently.

"The Priestess is upset," the first woman said loudly enough to be heard.

"I can't blame her," the second woman replied with a snort.

"I understand she is President Layan's daughter, but enough is enough. Why didn't the Priestess put the little brat in her place?"

"It's not that she had a choice."

"She's the Holy Priestess. Of course she has a choice!"

"In this case, she didn't."

"What do you mean?"

"Haven't you heard of…?"

"Haven't I heard of what?"

"There are some rumors… no?"

"No, what are you talking about?"

"There are some allegations about her celibacy—"

"Allegations about her Holiness' celibacy? What heresy is that? How can you say such things?"

"Well, I wasn't the one divulging such rumors! It was the brat who menaced to talk. I just heard of them."

"I don't believe it, not even for a second." The second woman sounded rather nervous. "And, you should be more careful with what you say around here." She paused for a long while, and then she added, "Anyway, not even the President's daughter should be able to ask for a baby as if it was a new toy. It's immoral that she wants to have a daughter without having married a nice woman first. If you ask me, she should be sent home with her tushy properly dusted."

"The Priestess thinks otherwise, obviously," the other woman answered dryly. "Anyway, everything is ready here. Call for the brat."

A few minutes passed without even the slightest sound. Then Mauricio heard loud steps walking past his room and into the other.

"Mistress, if you would, lie on this bed, please." The first woman had changed the tone of her voice considerably. Now she was all sweetness.

"Thank you, Ancilla Bettany," a third voice said. It sounded gentle and young.

"The Priestess will be here shortly. Now, I'm going to inject you with the sedative. You'll be asleep in a few minutes. Do you have any questions?" the second woman asked in the same sweet tone as the first.

"No, you were very exhaustive when you explained the process to me. I am ready to conceive with the help of the Priestess. Thank you for your patience, Ancilla Martha," the young woman said with a pleasant lilt in her voice.

"At your service, Mistress," both women said at the same time. Several steps echoed from the ventilation grid, along with metallic sounds, and finally, a door was closed with a gentle thump.

Mauricio stood with his back to the wall, staring at nothing, waiting to be summoned by the guard. A few minutes later, his eyes turned back to the ventilation grid, wishing that it was a window opening to the other room. Then something happened. The young woman started singing. He had never heard a woman singing before. Slaves usually sang at night when the darkness was too much to bear, and they sang during the day when the guards weren't paying much attention to them. But the singing he heard now was different. Apart from the obvious fact that a woman's voice is different from a man's, softer and sweeter, the girl was singing with joy and abandonment. She was happy to be alive. And she had a beautiful voice.

Mauricio had the absurd thought of wanting to see her. He knew it was ridiculous the moment it came to mind, but the thought kept nagging at him the whole time she sang. Her voice soared through the ventilation grid and came down to embrace Mauricio. She held one last note longer than he thought possible, and then she abruptly stopped.

"We're done with you," a guard, different from the one who had escorted him there, announced while opening the door.

Mauricio's ears were offended by the intrusion of the guard's scratchy voice. He couldn't shake the memory of the melody he had just heard.

"Move." The guard poked him with a long stick.

Mauricio focused his eyes on the woman and took a step toward the door. She looked like she was waiting for him to do something. He silently cursed the woman, but didn't give her any reason to vent her frustration on him. Instead, he memorized the route to his cell. They had made two right turns when the guard's pager started beeping loudly. She kept him at arm's length with the stick and paused to check the pager.

"Blast it." She reached for her cell phone and dialed a number with increasing worry on her face.

"Mariam reporting." The guard's voice was tightly controlled, but the hand holding the stick was moving around in wild circles. She muttered several sentences meant to sound obsequious and then listened for a few seconds while breathing heavily. She closed the cell phone with an angry look on her face.

Mauricio stood there, trying to blend into the wall and avoiding the guard's eyes. He had learned this trick when he was just a toddler. Normally it worked. He didn't even flinch when the circling stick almost connected with his cheekbone.

"Stay there." The guard opened a room on her left, ordered him inside and slammed the door behind him hastily.

Mauricio heard her stomping in the hallway, cursing out loud and complaining that she wasn't a fathered woman to be used as a fetching maid, not even for the blasted Priestess. And then, nothing. He was alone again, the door left ajar. He stared at the door, his mind running wild. The temptation was too great. Such opportunities didn't occur every day. On the other hand, the retribution for taking the opportunity would be high. If the guards caught him.

Mauricio's hand was on the door's handle before his brain could add anything to his already mixed thoughts. He walked down the hallway and had turned left twice already when he felt the first pang of worries knocking on his consciousness. He put aside the feeling immediately. He walked past the door of the room he had been in and went straight to the next door. He tested the handle. The door was unlocked. No sound came from inside. He looked over his shoulders. Nobody was coming. He took a deep breath and slowly opened the door. He cautiously peeked inside and stopped breathing altogether. The room was white, like the majority of the rooms in the facility, but it was filled from floor to ceiling with an array of machinery. In the middle of the room, almost hidden by the machinery, was a young woman lying on a bed.

Mauricio shouldn't have been surprised by the girl's presence. He knew a woman with a young voice had been singing in that room. If he took the time to consider what he was doing there, out of his designated room, he would have admitted that his curiosity to see the girl had won over his reasoning. Still, he was mesmerized by her. He had never looked twice at a woman before. His guards were interchangeable. Younger, older, fatter, slimmer, women all look the same to him: mean. The girl on the bed looked different. She was small with long, chestnut hair that trailed down the bed to the floor. Her face was minute with a little nose that turned slightly up at the end. Mauricio wondered what color her eyes were. Her skin was golden brown, while his was olive, and she was wearing the same green gown he was wearing. Somehow, she looked better in it than he did.

Mauricio didn't dare walk closer to the bed. He stood at a distance, looking at her from the door. She moved a finger of her outstretched hand and sighed while murmuring something incoherent. He unwillingly smiled at the singsong quality of her voice. Mauricio moved one timid step toward her. He raised his hand and, with a sudden decision, passed it through the curtain of her falling hair. He smiled again; this time he was fully conscious of the happiness he was feeling. A strand of hair caught between his fingers and he looked at it under the artificial white light. The hair changed color as he moved it this way and that. Mauricio let the hair fall through his fingers and bent lower to be at the same level of the girl's face. He could hear the breath coming in and out of her mouth. He moved closer to smell her skin. Mauricio inhaled her scent and smiled again. *You smell of something clean... and sweet.* He fought the urge to taste her.

The distant sound of several hurried steps froze him in midair. Mauricio sprang upright and to the door in one single movement. He checked that the hallway was still clear and ran away in the opposite direction from the approaching steps. He flew back to the room he left and sat on the floor. For several minutes, he could only hear his heart beating loudly against his chest. Then he realized that he was shaking uncontrollably. Finally, he saw that he had left the door open. Mauricio stretched one trembling leg and gently pushed the door until he heard a distinct click. When his heart slowed, he heard voices outside in the hallway.

"The Priestess said that the last deposit was enough. You can take him back to his cell. The brat is being treated right now." One guard was standing just outside the door.

"I can't wait to get rid of her. She's only causing problems. We had to double the surveillance. And on top of everything else, we are working two or three shifts per day, because of *Her-Royal-Pain-in-the-Ass'* presence," another guard commented.

"Playtime is over," one of the two guards announced. The key turned in the lock, closing the door instead of opening it. A second of hesitation and then the key turned the other way.

"Damn..." The guard immediately looked inside the cell.

"What is it?" the other asked with a suspicious tone.

"Nothing," the plump guard said after double-checking the slave was where she left him. She couldn't help but exhale rather loudly.

Thank the Heavens for small favors. Mauricio raised his eyes to the ceiling. If the guard who had forgotten to lock the door had been alone, he would now be at the receiving end of an unpleasant series of privileges that would guarantee him retaliation by the hand of the other less-fortunate slaves. As it was, the woman would never admit to the other guard of having done something so stupid. Forgetting to secure a slave meant losing their job. For some reason, the guards working around the Temple were particularly terrified of doing anything wrong. It was the subject of infinite speculation among the men.

The guard looked at him with wary eyes, but she didn't say anything.

You can't prove anything.

"I'll walk with you. I am headed to take another slave back, anyway," the other guard said.

"Great," the plump guard commented.

Later that night, in the privacy of his own cell, Mauricio's lips turned up, but he refrained from laughing. The room had only three solid walls. The fourth was a grid of metal bars. Mauricio wanted to tell his adventure to everybody who would listen. He wanted to be the one, for once, whom every other man listened to, but guards were always skulking around. It wasn't safe to push his luck, which he had just drained for the rest of the year. The stunt he pulled today was nowhere close to the other little acts of verbal rebellion he had tried on the guards. Instead of announcing to the world that he had defied orders and almost touched a woman, he kept smiling to himself. He had realized several years ago that he preferred to remain alive. A slave's life wasn't life at all, but Mauricio was attached to the little he had.

CHAPTER 3

For several nights after the encounter, he barely slept and constantly replayed the memories of the girl. He thought that if he kept thinking of her, her features would be etched forever in his mind and he would never forget how she looked or how she smelled. But memories are tricky companions and tend to betray one's heart.

Days and weeks passed. The guards had resumed their usual alertness. Cells were locked tightly and conversations were held away from the ventilation grids. He was asked to deposit his semen on a daily basis, and he complied as he always had over the years.

Mauricio felt alone for the first time in his life. For twenty-two years he had longed for acceptance; he had dreamed impossible dreams, despising his position as a slave with privileges. He had learned how to dull the pain he felt after the worst beatings. He had learned to live like a pariah among the other slaves and had even come to terms with the fact that fathered women would probably hate *him*. Not any other slave, just him. He, as a semental, was the reason fathered women were considered lesser beings by the pure breeds. Because of him, he had been told, his mother didn't have a soul.

When he finally realized that he wasn't going to see the girl again, his thoughts turned bleak, and he stopped caring about the flow of time. Not that, for a slave, the succession of days meant anything. Time for a man was a procession of similar activities constantly repeated over a lifetime. Mauricio, different from everybody else by choice, cared about the way he spent his existence. He knew the day would come when, after having helped with the creation of an army of fathered women and after having broken his back in the fields, he would end up in a retirement facility. No man had ever come back to tell what happened in the feared retirement facilities. It wasn't so hard to imagine why.

But, when that day came, Mauricio wanted to be sure that he had left a mark. Even if it was something small, it would be something nonetheless.

Then, the short-lived adrenaline rush had consumed him inside out and left him bereft of something he'd never had. He had tasted something he couldn't define and he had liked it. Mauricio collapsed under the wall of reality. What was left now was a hopeless life. He reached the peak of sadness when the guards came one morning and moved him to another wing of the facility. His new cell was smaller, colder, and most of all, it was far away from the field-workers' cells, closer to the laboratories where he went to make his deposits every day. Nobody had talked to him before, but at least he had enjoyed the men's voices at night. Now he only heard mechanical buzzing and metallic chirping.

One morning, after his usual monthly physical check, Mauricio was escorted deeper into the laboratory wing. He was used to the mercurial moods of the women and changes of plans were frequent. There could be several reasons for the unexpected stroll. Maybe the whole wing was being sterilized; the cleaning was long overdue. Mauricio hoped for a longer walk. He had woken up, with muscles stiffer than usual, and was feeling particularly blue. Any change in his routine was welcome. After a few minutes of brisk walking, not as long as he had wished for, he was shown inside a deposit room and told to stay put. Almost immediately, he had a sense of *déjà vu*. Voices were coming from the ventilation grid.

"How many viable female embryos do we have?" an older woman asked.

"We have at least three. One is particularly strong," another woman, maybe the doctor, answered after a few seconds.

"Excellent. Do you think we can start the procedure today?" the older woman asked with a satisfied tone.

"I don't see why not. I'm ready to implant the embryo as soon as the girl is here."

"I'll call *Her-Royal-Pain* immediately. The sooner we are done with her, the better."

Mauricio's mind filled in all the blanks in the conversation. *Keep talking*, he thought with renewed hope. *I need to know if you are talking about that girl I can't stop thinking about.* The only sounds that came through the vent were those of a leaking faucet. "Come back, please," he murmured to the ceiling, waiting for something to happen. *Would it kill you to please me, just once?* When it was clear that the women had left the adjacent room, he sat down and occupied his time tracing doodles on the dusty floor with his fingers; he found drawing relaxing. Some days he spent hours covering the window of his cell with intricate laces made from fingertips on moist glass. One warm breath on the windowpane and there was a whole new world of filigree designs; one brush with an open hand, and the canvas was ready for another masterpiece. Mauricio was good at finding ways to entertain himself.

In this room, all he had was the dust on the floor and his fingers. It was more than enough, but he couldn't concentrate on the task. Instead of drawing, Mauricio started playing with the frayed hem of his pants. He circled his finger around a loose thread and absentmindedly pulled at it one way and the other. Finally, a thin strip of fabric gave away. Meanwhile he kept analyzing the words he had heard. With restless hands, he played some more with the strip of fabric and then went back to the drawing activity. When he took a distracted look at the design on the floor, Mauricio saw a half-finished, delicate profile. The sound of steps came from outside his room. He hastily stood up and erased the drawing with his foot. The steps didn't pause at his door.

"At what time do I have to prep the room, Doctor?" a woman asked.

"The President's daughter's procedure is scheduled at noon. Have everything ready by eleven," a second woman answered.

"It will be done by eleven, then." A clicking sound accompanied the words.

"Thanks, Ancilla." The doctor's voice was barely audible. Then nothing else.

Almost at the same time, the door in Mauricio's room opened and the plump guard, who had become some sort of personal escort lately, made a gesture to him, indicating that it was time to go back to his cell. Mauricio wanted to know why he had been forgotten there, but he knew better than to ask. He followed the guard outside silently. Out of boredom, he decided to memorize the route they were taking. Two turns left, three turns right. Two different hallways. One hundred and thirty-two steps from the room that was being prepared for the President's daughter to his cell. Give or take.

Meanwhile, Mauricio noticed the commotion disturbing the quiet of the laboratories wing. There were more guards than usual scurrying about. Doors opened and closed, revealing the activities inside. Mauricio saw other sementals waiting for their turns to be brought back to their cells. So, the hypothesis that their wing was being sanitized was probably correct. It had been sheer luck that he had ended up in *that* deposit room twice.

The plump guard didn't even look at him. *Good, I get the silent treatment today*, Mauricio thought. Pure breed guards came in two different types: the ones who would never acknowledge a slave's presence if they could help it, and the ones who draw great pleasure in tormenting men. The plump guard oscillated between the two types depending on the day. *Keep minding your business and we'll both have something to be pleased about today.* He blended with the walls while the woman made several phone calls. *I'm not here. I'm not here; you can talk as much as you want.*

The plump guard seemed to be following his mental suggestion. "Today, if we are lucky, the whole shenanigan should end. Let's hope that the brat can keep the baby, and that the President isn't going to shut us down when she finds out." The woman paused for a moment to let three busy-looking guards pass them.

"No, no... the Priestess has personally chosen the best semental we have here to match the brat's long list of requirements..." The woman involuntarily shot a sideway look at Mauricio.

Don't mind me, keep talking, he thought, flattening against the wall.

"You can't believe how detailed her list was. The brat wants a baby girl with brown or green eyes; light-brown, straight hair; olive skin, not too dark, not too pale. Ah, and I almost forgot that she also wants her daughter to grow taller than she is and with long limbs." She snorted at the last comment.

This baby is going to look just like me. For some reason Mauricio liked that idea.

"And this is just a superficial recount of what the brat asked. She was in that room for hours writing down every single insignificant detail about her perfect baby girl. Fortunately, we have a semental that fits the bill almost to perfection. Even the facial features are similar to what she asked. Straight nose, big almond-shaped eyes... No, I am not kidding! She went so far as to draw the shape of the mouth."

Why would they need a semental? The girl is a pure breed. They don't need me for that. He was getting more and more interested in the conversation. *I can't' believe this cow is talking like this in front of me. And the women think we're the stupid ones.*

The guard paused for a second, listening to the other person's comments and then she answered a question Mauricio couldn't hear, "The Priestess didn't want to take the chance of having to repeat this... I know, it would be a disaster." Another group of guards invaded the hallway with a machine on wheels composed of a big cylinder towering a medical bed. The plump guard shut up immediately and covered the phone with her hands.

"Sorry, the doctor is moving the OR to the second floor, and the medical guards are running wild through the whole place. You never know who is listening," the guard said to the cell phone as soon as the hallway cleared.

Me, for example?

"Love you too." She finished her conversation and directed Mauricio inside his cell at the same time.

"Hey, Lina!" Another guard approached with a big smile.

"Oh, hey, Carla! Long time no see. How have you been?" The plump guard turned around to greet the other woman.

Mauricio acted on impulse. Without thinking, he put the strip of torn fabric he was still holding over the cell door's lock. The plump guard pulled on the door and waited for the click announcing that the lock had slid into place. The click came, rather muted by the fabric, but loud enough for the guard to leave without double-checking.

Mauricio heard the two women's voices getting softer until they disappeared altogether. He waited a few minutes and then gently wiggled the piece of fabric to move the lock. Another faint sound announced that the lock had just been dislodged from its side. Mauricio wiggled the fabric some more, hoping that nobody was outside. The door opened imperceptibly. Mauricio peeked outside cautiously and then gently pulled the door back out, being careful to leave it opened.

Satisfied with the result, Mauricio took a deep breath. The girl who had taken permanent residence inside his mind was here. And he was going to see her again. The possible outcome didn't scare Mauricio. He didn't think for a second that he could get caught. He only wanted another glimpse at her. As simple as that. *I should hate you*, he thought. *Or at least be repulsed by your sight. You are lovely, I must admit... but still a woman. You belong to the wrong sex: your race has doomed me to slavery.*

After taking a good look outside, Mauricio left his cell as if it was the most natural thing to do. He ducked and took cover behind corners every time he heard approaching noises. He made it through all the way to his final destination without surprises. It helped that the guards didn't expect any slave to act the way Mauricio was acting. It also helped that he wasn't thinking at all. Otherwise, fear would have frozen him in the act of opening a door he shouldn't even be close to.

If the door opens, it's meant to be. Mauricio turned the handle and then pushed gently. The door swung on its hinges and opened with a whoosh. *It's a sign I am not doing anything wrong.* He closed his eyes before taking a look inside. *I hope she's here.* She was there. Still sleeping. Still small. The girl was connected to several machines that beeped regularly; she was cradled in a cocoon of wires and covered in needles. *She seems... happy.* He had never seen a face so peaceful. The men he knew were bitter in the soul and beaten in the body. They were never happy. The women he had the unfortunate luck to interact with were always complaining about having to work with the slaves. They rarely smiled, even to each other.

Mauricio smiled. He truly smiled, for no apparent reason at all. His mouth moved without his knowledge. It rearranged the muscles in his face in a fashion that was foreign to him. He walked toward the bed, still grinning. She turned her head and a strand of her hair covered her right eye. Mauricio reached out and moved the strand out of the way. His fingers barely grazed her skin, but she turned toward his hand. He stepped back, worried that she was going to wake up.

"Thanks," she murmured in her dreams, her voice a whisper. She sighed contently and sank into a deeper sleep.

Mauricio's smile widened. *I like your voice.* There was something refreshing about it—a gentle quality he wasn't accustomed to hearing in a woman's voice. He realized that she had never actually talked to *him*, but he didn't want to think too much about that. He wished she would sing again. *What color are your eyes? I really want to see them.* Mauricio was taken by a sudden impulse and acted on it. Lately, he was having a lot of those moments, he realized. He moved to the side of the bed and sat beside it on the only chair present in the room. He took her right hand in his and stroked her skin with light fingers.

Mauricio couldn't help but notice the unblemished quality of her complexion against his. His hands were bigger than hers, marred by scars, and dirty. That last realization made him drop her hand on the bed immediately. He tried to clean the palm of his hands on his pants.

"You're warm," the girl said without opening her eyes. Her hand seemed to search for the warmth that had abandoned it.

Mauricio tentatively nudged his fingers close to hers. She grabbed his hand and smiled. He would have stayed there, still as a statue for the rest of his life. There was so much peace in the warmth of that gesture. He knew she wasn't holding him. *I want to be that person you're dreaming about.* Mauricio felt sadness creep in his heart. *Why wasn't I born a pure breed?* he thought, even though he knew he should hate them. But he wanted to feel this good again more than he wanted to hate his captors. And the thought by itself was maddening. *Hate is the only meaningful feeling when you are a slave. It keeps you alive. It keeps you strong.*

Mauricio removed his hand slowly, conscious that he had soiled the white linen surrounding her delicate fingers. One of the machines connected to her left hand started beeping. He knew that it was time to make an exit. The girl's lips were slightly parted and Mauricio saw the white of her teeth. There were so many things he wanted to ask her. And he was still curious about the color of her eyes.

The girl granted Mauricio's wish right when he decided it was wise to leave. He was retracing his steps toward the door, carefully avoiding the snarl of cables entangled on the floor, but allowed himself one last glance at her, when she presented him with the most beautiful set of dark brown eyes. The girl stared at him in confusion for a few seconds.

"Oh my—" Mauricio lost control of his dexterity and his right foot became entangled in the cables. He thrashed around, his arms outstretched to break the fall and a machine went down with him. Mauricio realized one second too late that the transparent pipe that went flying along with the machine was attached to a needle in the girl's left arm. As it was yanked out, her eyes grew wide, and then she screamed at the top of her lungs.

"It's okay; I'm not going to hurt you. I'd never hurt you. Please, keep it quiet," Mauricio said, horrified by her reaction. The girl screamed louder. Mauricio stood there, thinking of the best way to calm her and lost precious moments he should have used to escape. He moved a step closer to the bed and the girl's eyes reflected how terrified she was of him. Mauricio felt a sting of pain that wasn't physical and he jumped back toward the door as if a jolt of electricity had shot through his body.

A moment later, a nurse appeared at the door. "Mistress, what's wrong?" the woman asked and then screamed when she saw Mauricio. Her hand reached for a button on the wall. "I need help. There is a man inside the room!" she yelled loudly at an intercom that had started pulsing red.

"Stop where you are. Don't move," the nurse ordered Mauricio. She looked at him with a mixture of fear and disgust, and then she seemed to remember something. She fished in her apron's pocket, and from the look in her eyes, she found what she was looking for.

"Don't move," she said again before aiming a Taser at Mauricio.

CHAPTER 4

I must be alive. Mauricio woke up with one of the worst headaches of his life. It took him several minutes to get his bearings, and even when he did, he couldn't be sure of how he was faring. His body was aching everywhere, and after a cursory inspection, he found that the left side of his face was swollen. "I'm sure it could be worse," he said just to hear his own voice.

When he tried to stretch his muscles, he realized that his left leg was shackled to the wall. *Where am I now?* He wasn't in his cell, from the little he could see in the dim light. He hadn't slept on a bed, hard or otherwise, but on a wet floor. "I'm not going to look down, I'm not going to look down", he repeated, but he did look down and immediately regretted it. .

Then, finally, when the fog had cleared, he wondered why. *Why am I still alive after the nurse found me in the girl's room?* It just didn't make sense that his life had been spared. *Unless what they want to do to me is worse than death.* Mauricio shuddered with foreboding. The girl was the President's daughter, after all. He shouldn't be alive.

No, he thought with terrifying clarity. *It isn't as simple as that.* The nurse had Tasered a slave who was attempting violence against the President's daughter. The girl had been screaming as if he was attempting to hurt her. His only hope was a quick death.

Mauricio was left in that dark cell so long, time simply ceased to have any meaning. The only interaction with other human beings was thrice a day when the guards brought him food. The women were under orders not to speak to him, for any reason. When they were around him, the guards didn't even speak to each other.

He was permitted a few minutes of walking every other day, the only physical activity he was allowed. The women never beat him, and the food, although bland, wasn't disgusting, but the isolation almost did him in.

Time passed; the shackles anchoring him to the wall were removed; the pain became bearable.

Mauricio realized one day how long he had been confined there when he ran his hand through his hair and found that he could tie it in a ponytail. He still didn't have a clue why the women hadn't killed him already. The longer they left him there to rot, the more his imagination ran wild, conjuring tales of such horror that once or twice he broke into tears.

Finally, the day came when his future would be revealed.

Nobody told him anything, but the electricity in the air was palpable. He could see from his cell the guards moving around purposefully. The metal bars prevented him from sticking his head out when nobody was close, but he saw enough. And what he saw gave him pause.

Maybe dying isn't that bad, he morosely thought. *If I'm lucky, being dead is a permanent state.* Compared to what the guards wanted to do to him, it was probably the best option. *Maybe it's just a bad dream, and I'll wake up any moment now.*

When an older woman appeared before the metal bars of his cell, his worst fear took shape. He noticed that she was wearing a billowy, colored dress and a headpiece. The older woman raised one hand and several golden armbands slid down her arm. The gesture meant something because several guards appeared at her side.

He nervously tugged the rigid collar around his neck. He felt oddly reassured by the tingling sensation bordering on pain, but it also meant that he wasn't having a nightmare.

"Please, kill me as fast as possible," Mauricio pleaded. He knew it was a useless attempt, but he couldn't help it. He would have killed himself if he had a way.

The older woman looked at him with mild distaste and a great deal of curiosity. "Clean him and bring him to the lab," the woman said to someone else out of Mauricio's sight. He thought that the request was odd. If they were going to torture him to death, why bother with a clean body? Mauricio looked on quietly from his corner while the cell was opened, and he stood still as one of the guards came closer, hooking a chain to his collar. He finally followed the guards outside without attempting any other conversation. Nothing he could say would make the slightest difference in any case.

The elegant, older woman led the small army of guards ahead. Mauricio tried to straighten his body, but the muscles in his legs were trembling, and the guard holding the chain yanked him forward several times, making it impossible for him to keep up. After a few minutes of walking, he started seeing dark spots on the wall and fell twice, annoying the guard. He stood up immediately after she struck him with a short whip.

"What are you doing? You're damaging the semental," the older woman said without turning around. Mauricio wondered how she knew. "Don't strike him again or he'll faint, and I need him awake," she added, shaking her arm with a distinct sound of bells.

"Apologies, Priestess," the guard said. And then added under her breath, "He doesn't walk fast enough. What am I supposed to do?" She gave him a vicious tug. "Don't make a single noise, or I'll come visit you later."

Mauricio distractedly made the mental connection between the older woman leading him to his death and the Priestess who had been mentioned by the guards before. *I finally make your acquaintance*, he thought.

"Give him something to eat, before you take him to the deposit room." The Priestess disappeared behind a door opening like a square of light into the dark and cold hallway.

Mauricio was utterly confused; he didn't understand what was happening and that scared him even more.

The guard used the chain as a leash and pulled him inside another room. "Wash your sorry self and do it fast."

I could use a shower, he thought. *Water isn't hot, but it isn't cold either; it could be worse*, he tried to convince himself. Mauricio massaged his muscles to ease the tingles of pain shooting through his legs and arms. The water wasn't warm enough to ease his aching muscles or do any good other than cleansing his skin. In any case, he wouldn't have been able to relax even if the water had been hot. Mauricio took the shower with his back to the wall, keeping an eye on the guard. The suspense of not knowing what they were going to do to him was wearing him out. Finally, the guard told him to stop. She gave him just enough time to dry what he could of his body with a small towel and then pointed one finger at a corner. Mauricio understood the order and waited for what was next.

"Eat." The guard dropped his food in front of him.

Mauricio wasn't hungry. Since the three meals a day he had been receiving weren't large, he should have been starving. He had even lost weight. But the impending death sentence wasn't doing miracles for his appetite. He sat on the floor and ate what he could, anyway. There was no point in arguing with a guard. The gooey porridge stuck in his throat, and he choked.

"Drink." The guard promptly poured some water in a metal bowl.

How humane of you, Mauricio thought while drinking the water from the bowl. He didn't give her the satisfaction to gulp it. He had very few things left in his life, but one of those was pride. He fervently hoped that when the moment came, he could withstand torture with the same spirit. By the time he had finished with his meal, Mauricio was so nervous that his stomach started clenching.

"I think you are refreshed enough. Back to work." The guard yanked his chain and dragged him outside and into the hallway again.

"Move, idiot. And to think that the little brat needs *you!*" The guard seemed truly annoyed with Mauricio. He was too taken aback by her last words to pay any attention to her mood. The guard didn't feel sympathetic to his woolgathering and kicked him in the shin. He howled in pain; she had been careful to hit him with the reinforced tip of her boot.

Heavens forbid any more personal contact, like a sane, old-fashioned slap.

"I warned you," the guard said, satisfied that the slave was finally moving at her pace.

But, I haven't said anything! He remembered the woman's earlier threat.

She opened a door and let Mauricio in. "Go and do what you are supposed to do. You know the drill." The guard took a last, disgusted look at him and then closed the door behind her.

"At least they need me for something," Mauricio said under his breath. He gave a brief look at the room and then sat on the plastic chair waiting for him in the corner. The familiar transparent cup was there as well. Mauricio shook his head in disbelief. *What is that supposed to mean?* He thought about several scenarios and came out with one that was at least plausible. The women needed him for one last deposit. The fact remained that the President's daughter had been mentioned, again. Mauricio couldn't find any possible explanation for that girl needing him for anything. She was the purest of the pure breeds. And pure breeds only used sementals to conceive fathered women. But, now that he was thinking about it and connecting the dots—the plump guard, the nurses, the doctor—all of them had hinted at some sort of connection between the brat, as they called her, and him. It was true that he had only heard bits and pieces of scattered conversations, but the fact that he was still alive kind of validated his current train of thoughts. But he realized the little he knew and thought he understood about the world he lived in was probably wrong. Loud tapping on the door startled Mauricio, who was far away from completing his task.

"The Priestess doesn't have time to waste," the guard yelled.

"Give me a moment," Mauricio grunted back, but kept his voice low. His mind was spinning with ideas, one wilder than the next, and his stomach was still painfully clenched. He still didn't know what plans they had for him. How was he supposed to fill the blasted cup, if he couldn't muster the right frame of mind?

"Done yet?" The guard was pounding on the door, again.

"I can't," Mauricio finally said, loud enough this time to be heard outside.

"What do you mean you can't? The Priestess is waiting for you!" The guard opened the door with an angry kick. "Do it now!

I order you." The woman's face was becoming red at an alarming rate.

"I can't," Mauricio repeated. *What are you, deaf and stupid?*

"I will kill you for disobeying me—" The guard impulsively took her gun from the holster and aimed at him.

"Stop!" someone outside the door said. The guard froze when she heard the imperious voice.

"Did you forget my orders?"

"Apologies, Your Holiness. I was only trying to teach him a lesson." The guard turned around to face the Priestess, who was now towering over her.

"I explicitly said that I wanted this semental unharmed. Did I, or did I not?" The Priestess looked stern. "You have been working with them for a lifetime, supposedly. Don't you know a thing or two about their flawed physiology?" The Priestess asked.

The guard cowered under the woman's cold stare. "I thought he was just wasting your precious time, Your Holiness. Please, accept my apologies, again," she whispered, kneeling on the floor.

It suits you well, you bitch, he thought, forgetting for a moment his own predicament.

"Listen well, all of you," the Priestess looked outside the door, where a few guards were waiting for her orders. "Sementals should be treated differently from the other slaves. *This* semental in particular, *must* be treated differently from the others. Are we clear?" She paused to let the information sink in. "Are we clear?" the Priestess repeated, raising her already booming voice when the guards didn't answer back; they looked terrified, but a unanimous chorus followed soon after. Everybody was perfectly clear about the semental in question.

"Now, I want him in a new cell." The Priestess shot a last look at the guard and then turned her head to address the rest of the group. "Make sure you don't kill him until I order so, or you'll follow his fate." Then the Priestess did something Mauricio wasn't expecting. She looked at him. Her eyes locked his in a stare that sent shivers down his spine, and then she turned to face the guards again. "You should be thankful that a slave tested your security system. At least *I* realized my guards aren't *guarding* enough."

He stood there in his corner, hoping that she would leave soon. He wanted to faint. The *Holy Priestess* had looked at *him* and he was still alive. The realization that he wasn't going to be killed any time soon hit him hard. He felt a physical blow to his stomach and vomited the entire meager, gooey meal on the floor.

"You'll take better care of the sementals under your jurisdiction." The Priestess didn't flinch at the spectacle. She just stepped aside and left, after giving another pitiful look at the guard whose face was greener than Mauricio's.

Mauricio found that he liked his new cell. *The floor is dry; there isn't mold on the wall; it isn't cold; and the bed isn't a slab of hard rock*, he thought when he took stock of the place. *And, what is that? A window?* It was a small rectangular hole in the wall with metal bars, but he had never had a window in any of his cells before and thought it was the most beautiful thing. During the first week in his new residence, he spent all of his time staring at the light coming from outside. *Outside. I wish I could see what's beyond this wall.* He imagined the sun illuminating the field workers' long days. He had heard the men complaining about rain and wind, but he couldn't understand what they meant. Images of beautiful, colorful things formed in his mind. He only knew life inside a series of dark cells that had changed from time to time—sometimes they were warmer, sometimes colder, but they remained always the same: colorless. He longed for colors and fresh air.

Mauricio looked at the window high on the wall, wishing he could move his bed closer to use as a step, but it was bolted on the floor. *Great view, nonetheless.* The light changed constantly during the day and disappeared at night. Mauricio never grew tired of looking at the way the light moved on the floor from one corner of his small cell to the other. Sometimes the light was brighter, especially in the morning, other times it was warm and yellow. From the open window, the outside world slowly started pouring inside, and Mauricio discovered what the wind felt like when it blew through the metal bars. *It's not that bad,* he thought. *I like the sound of it.* He also grew accustomed to the whispers of the field workers coming back at night. *Today was good—they seem happy,* or, *Today wasn't great—they are complaining more than usual.* He started assessing the day depending on the field workers' mood.

He came to enjoy the singing of the birds first thing in the morning, and after a while, he was even able to recognize the sound of droplets of rain hitting the outside wall. And, once, the wind brought the rain inside his cell. He touched the small, wet tears and laughed. *I wish I could walk outside and be drenched by it, so I'd know how it feels on my skin.*

Then, one night, another sound was channeled inside his cell—a voice he dreamed of every waking moment. Mauricio would have recognized her voice among a chorus of feminine ones, but she sang alone that night and every night after that. The first time he heard her, Mauricio thought he was dreaming. The girl's voice was as crystalline and fresh as he remembered. She sang lullabies, and sometimes she told children's tales with her soft voice. Mauricio knew what lullabies and tales were because of his father; her songs took him back to the time when he was just a scared little boy and his father soothed his fears with his voice. Mauricio cried for several nights, remembering everything he had lost, and he hated her for that.

But, every morning, he woke up with a longing he had never felt before. She made him sad with her songs, but she also made him feel alive. He couldn't get enough of that high. For once in his life, he had something to look forward to. Every day, long after the field workers had come back for their daily rest, when the square of light on his wall became a soft shade of yellow and then disappeared, Mauricio waited for her. She normally came out as soon as the darkness filled his cell. Mauricio could hear her short steps, light on the gravel, and after a few minutes, she would start tuning her voice with several scales. He thought that the girl had the most beautiful voice in the whole world.

One night, Mauricio impatiently waited for the darkness to enclose his cell, but the girl didn't come. He stood there, thinking that every second lasted an hour and hoping to hear her steps breaking the silence. His eyes started watering and his head lolled to one side, but he still waited. He woke up the next morning, sore and crouched on the floor in the same position he had been sitting in. His mood didn't improve during the day and he failed to comply with his only task.

The guard assigned to him, a tall and wispy brunette, the new face who had replaced the one the Priestess had rebuked publicly, didn't beat him—Priestess' orders—but managed to let half of his lunch fall on the floor of his cell.

I won't give you the pleasure to see me on all fours, scooping my meal off the ground. He slowly ate what was left on the plate; then he looked at the guard in defiance. His stomach was aching with hunger, but he sat on the bed and let the food go bad before his eyes. His dinner portion was even smaller than lunch. Mauricio didn't say anything. As a slave, he could only control the way he accepted the adversities dealt him.

The square of light moved on the floor of Mauricio's cell and his heart started pounding. When the air became colder and the night bugs started chirping and clicking, he could barely stand still. He stood up and sat down dozens of times. Finally, the first shades of the night obscured the cell's walls. Mauricio forced his body to stay still. Seconds, minutes, hours, all passed in a painful silence, but he refused to admit that he was going to spend the night alone again. Hours later, hungry and tired, he laid his head on the bed and started singing softly to lessen his pain. The following day was a replay of the first one. He didn't fill the transparent cup. The tall guard was annoyed. His stomach paid the consequences.

The third night came and Mauricio lay on his bed and closed his eyes tightly. When the square of light passed on his face and then disappeared beyond the wall, he felt the ache rise in his chest. He was also lightheaded. He had eaten close to nothing in the last two days and the pain devouring his stomach was growing stronger. Mauricio started singing, as he had the night before, and he lost himself in the act.

"You have a beautiful voice," the girl said from outside.

At first Mauricio thought he was imagining things. Hunger did that to him sometimes. He was also very tired and his eyes didn't want to open. He turned to one side of the bed and resumed singing.

"Where did you learn how to sing so well?" the girl asked.

Mauricio fought to open his eyes and sat on the bed. His head swayed one way and the other.

"You are a slave," the girl said.

Mauricio thought that it was the stupidest thing to say. *I have a man's voice. What else can I be, if not a slave?*

"I'm not going to report you, if you talk to me." The girl sounded cheerful.

Mauricio couldn't believe this conversation was happening, but he could hear his heart beating in his throat already.

"I really like your voice. I wouldn't do anything to put you in any trouble," the girl said, seriously now.

"I like your voice, too," Mauricio managed to say in a whisper.

"What did you say?" the girl asked and her voice sounded closer. She was probably standing right under the wall of Mauricio's cell.

"I like to hear you sing," Mauricio said slightly louder.

"When did you hear me?"

"Every night you sing... except for the last two nights." Mauricio hoped he hadn't said too much.

"I was sick," she explained.

"Oh... I hope you're better now." *What can I say to you?* He had never had a conversation with a woman before. *I don't even know how to speak to another man, for Heavens' sake.* The only person he had exchanged words with regularly had been his father, and he had loved him and protected him. But his heart was beating faster and he really hoped that she would keep talking to him.

"I am, thank you. What were you singing?" she asked after a long pause, as if she was deciding what to say to him.

"A song my father taught me when I was a boy."

"What does it say?"

"It's a kid's song." He was surprised by her question.

"I don't know the language of the song."

"It's about a man talking to his little kid." Mauricio had never thought until that moment that women wouldn't understand his father's language. Maybe he shouldn't have said anything. A long lost memory of his father telling him to be cautious when speaking their language around women resurfaced.

"It's... beautiful." Her voice broke a little. "What does the word *pax* mean? You said it several times."

"Peace; the father wants his kid to live in peace," he answered without thinking, despite what he had just remembered.

"I would like to hear some more," she said softly.

Mauricio couldn't believe the girl had asked him to sing for her. She was talking to him as if he were another woman. Although he couldn't be sure of how women talked among themselves. He knew that she wasn't talking to him as a man, in any case. The realization was so shocking that he lost the use of his tongue for several minutes.

"I already told you; I am not going to call the guards if you talk to me."

"But you did last time!" Mauricio couldn't help to retort and then regretted it immediately.

"What?" The girl sounded confused by his outburst. "No! I can't believe it... you are the slave who was found in my room three months ago?" She was genuinely surprised, but not angry. "It's okay, as I already said, twice, I am not calling for help. The last time I saw you, I screamed because I was coming out of the anesthesia. You have to admit that your presence in my room was rather upsetting." Her tone was calm.

"I'm sorry if I scared you. It wasn't my intention," he said defensively.

"I know. I saw the recording of what happened that day. You were very... gentle."

"I only wanted to see you."

"Why?"

"I have heard you sing before, and I wanted to see what you looked like." Mauricio felt a strange urge of telling the truth, even if he knew he was playing with fire.

"You heard me before?"

"I was left in a depository room next to yours. Sound traveled through the wall."

"What's a depository room?"

Mauricio was taken aback by this question. How was it possible that she didn't know?

"You can't say?" she pressed.

"No, it's not that. I thought you knew. It's a place the guards bring me to fill my quota of semen for the day," he said slowly.

"What do you mean?" The girl seemed interested.

"I am a semental." Mauricio thought that the name itself was enough explanation without having to be any more detailed.

"What does a semental do?" she asked instead.

Mauricio groaned. He really didn't want to say anything else about the topic. The other men had always treated him like the plague for being a semental. He didn't think that she was going to regard him any better. Maybe that explained why she was talking to him. She didn't know who he was and what he did for the guards.

"Guards use my semen to create fathered women," he said and his voice was angry. *Happy now?* he thought.

"Oh! I didn't know." The girl's voice came as a barely audible whisper.

"It's not that I like doing it. I have no choice," Mauricio said defensively and hurt.

"I studied physiology at school, but they didn't explain to us how things work in detail. I didn't know that there were particular slaves who... do only that," she said in a conciliatory tone.

He was astonished by her ignorance and, most of all, by the fact that she hadn't run away by now.

"You seem different from the other slaves," she said, surprising him even more.

Mauricio didn't know what to say after that. He didn't even know if she had meant it as a compliment. Probably not. Women didn't compliment slaves.

"In the recording, you stood there, watching me sleep. It felt like you were protecting me," she continued.

He was completely at loss for words.

"I must go now." The girl concluded her soliloquy without adding anything else.

Mauricio heard her steps moving away and wondered what had just happened. *I just had a conversation with a woman.* He kept thinking about that all night, playing the exchange over and over again. When the tall guard came to pick him up, he was still dazed by the events of the night before. He also hadn't slept at all and he felt hunger beyond bearing, but he smiled at the tall woman who still regarded him with disdain. He followed her to the depository room and even managed to fill the cup as requested. He didn't make it back to his cell, though. Black spots danced before his eyes when he stood up and then fainted.

CHAPTER 5

"What did I tell you regarding *this* semental?" Several voices talking at the same time woke Mauricio up, but only the Priestess' voice overpowered all the others. He lay quietly and awaited his fate, while trying to assess where he was. The place was unfamiliar—too clean and too bright. He half closed his eyes, too curious to shut them down, but cautious enough not to let the women know he had come around.

"Your Holiness, I was just following the rules. The slave wasn't producing at all, and I punished him by giving him less to eat," the tall guard said.

Mauricio, even lying down, was still lightheaded. He followed the conversation, thinking the whole situation would have been rather amusing if the women hadn't been talking about the propriety of starving him to death.

The Priestess shook her head. "You obviously don't understand, do you? You can't reduce his food without asking my permission." She was talking exceedingly slow, accentuating every word.

"My apologies, Your Holiness. I thought that... the handbook says to punish slaves if... but I realize now I should have known better given that he is—" The tall guard lowered her head to stare at the floor when the Priestess raised one hand to silence her.

"You are demoted, immediately." The Priestess' voice was calm. "From now on, I will personally hire all guards for the semental wing." She was now talking to another guard.

"As you wish, Your Holiness." The guard, a woman Mauricio hadn't seen before, lowered her head in deference.

"What I wish is to have guards with an education for a change. How can you hire someone who doesn't know anything about slaves?" the Priestess asked the audience, betraying her anger.

"Did you, at least, give him his daily ration of water?" She singled out the tall guard, who was trying to disappear near the back of the room.

The tall guard briefly looked at the Priestess, her face twisted in a terrified expression. "I'm... not sure..." she answered, voice broken.

"You aren't sure, or you know you didn't give him his daily ration of water?" The Priestess' voice boomed in the room.

"I might have... reduced the water."

"Have you even read the handbook you mentioned? Do you know what it says regarding withholding water?"

"I..." The tall guard began sobbing.

"Get her out of here. I can't bear stupidity." The Priestess waited as the woman was escorted outside, then looked around, giving each and every guard left in the room a piercing stare and then continued, "The handbook clearly states that it is critical, I repeat, critical *not* to reduce the amount of water allotted daily to slaves. The slave's productivity suffers from lack of water in their bodies. Semen production suffers without proper hydration. Now, do you have the slightest idea of what I am trying to say here?" She paused and low murmurs filled the silence.

Mauricio heard the words 'this semental', 'the President's daughter', and 'semen' repeated several times by the scared guards.

"Exactly! I see that you aren't completely useless. So, my question is, if the President's daughter loses the baby, what are we going to do without his semen?" the Priestess stated.

At the Priestess' words, Mauricio almost revealed he was full awake and listening. *This isn't possible... what she's saying... did I hear correctly?*

"I need him fully functional, and quickly. Give him something to hydrate him and, instead of three meals, give him six small meals today." The Priestess wrote down her instruction and passed the tablet to a nurse.

Mauricio's stomach started rumbling on cue; he was relieved when the Priestess left without having looked at him once the whole time. A nurse took his vitals and then punched his skin with a needle that was connected to a pipe that led to a bag full of a transparent fluid. Mauricio saw the liquid substance dripping inside the pipe, drop by drop, until it reached the needle. He couldn't help gasping when the cold liquid started pouring inside him. The feeling was, at first, unpleasant, but after few minutes, Mauricio noticed that he could think better. The fog that had swamped his thoughts was clearing fast. The nurse took his vitals again, read the numbers on a display at the end of his bed, and nodded, satisfied. She fussed over the machines in the room, waited until all the liquid in the bag had found its way inside Mauricio's body, hooked another full bag with a different liquid substance to the pipe and then left.

He soon felt better than he had in a month and was ready to go back to his cell. He didn't like the room he was in. It smelled of that clean, citrus scent that, in Mauricio's mind, was connected with that day, four years earlier, when the women had chosen him to be a semental. He was fully immersed in his memories when the door opened and a woman came in. Out of habit, he lowered his head and closed his eyes. Years of servitude had shaped him like that.

"I heard that you fainted," a familiar feminine voice said with a hint of concern. Mauricio opened his eyes and saw the girl looking at him. She walked toward his bed but stopped when she realized that she was too close to him. "How are you now?" the girl asked.

"Better. This water is miraculous." Mauricio raised his hand to show her the needle and the pipe with the light green substance dripping down.

"I tried it, too. It's good stuff," she said and then laughed.

Mauricio felt a foreign satisfaction at the fact that she was laughing. He didn't understand why it meant something to him, but it did. "What's your name?" he asked suddenly.

"Rose. But everybody calls me Rosie. What's yours?" If she was surprised by his question, she didn't show it.

"My dad used to call me Mauricio." His voice broke. He hadn't expected her to be interested in knowing his name. He had been a string of twelve digits for the last twenty-two years and had hated that number ever since a guard had made him memorize it.

"What a unique name." Rosie seemed to think about it for a few seconds and then said, "I like the sound of it."

"I like your name, too." Mauricio said, feeling that, as replies went, this wasn't the greatest.

"My mom has a penchant for flowers." Rosie was playing with her hands.

Mauricio thought the way her fingers toyed with a ring on her right hand was nice.

"I don't know anything about flowers," Mauricio said automatically, his eyes lingering on her hands.

"Oh—" Rosie looked at him with wide eyes and then said, "A rose is a flower with many petals that comes in different colors."

"It must be nice to look at." He slowly raised his head.

"Yes, roses are the prettiest flowers and they also smell wonderful."

"What's it like?" His eyes were now openly staring at her.

"A rose smells like sweet and spice, and sometimes also like dew. When I was born, my moms planted hundreds of roses under my bedroom's window, and when the buds opened I could smell the perfume drifting to my bed; their scent was almost intoxicating at night."

"I'd like that..." *To sit at night with you, surrounded by roses.* His heart made a somersault in his chest, his lungs suddenly seeking air. *Is this what feels like to be intoxicated?*

"You'd love it."

"I'm sure."

"I—" She silently looked at Mauricio for a few seconds before lowering her head. Her ring slipped from her finger and fell to the floor, sliding toward Mauricio's bed.

He reached for it at the same time she did, and for a moment, their hands touched. "Here," he said, placing the ring on her palm.

"Thanks. I should be more careful with this. It has the Layans crest on it," Rosie explained. When he didn't say anything back, she added, "It's my family ring." She waited for him to acknowledge her words, but he wasn't looking at the ring anymore.

"Just beautiful," he commented, his eyes now firmly on her.

"Thanks," she repeated.

Mauricio would have sworn that she was blushing.

"What happened to you?" she asked, changing topic abruptly.

"I haven't eaten a lot in the last three days," he said drily.

"You didn't want to eat?"

"I've been really hungry." Mauricio wanted to laugh.

Rosie's eyes widened in understanding and she blushed even deeper. "I didn't mean to offend you." She came closer to Mauricio.

"Don't worry." He was affected by her proximity.

"I forget how things are for... you." Rosie put a hand on his bed without touching him.

Mauricio wanted to move his hand and touch hers again, but doing so on purpose was unthinkable. He didn't dare change his position on the small frame of the bed.

"Sometimes I think that Ginecea should be different. I don't understand why things are the way they are."

Mauricio looked at her, transfixed. He couldn't believe what she was saying.

"You are the President's daughter!" Mauricio exclaimed.

"How do you know?"

"I overheard the guards talking about you." Mauricio remained vague on purpose.

"Oh, I can imagine the things they say." Rosie laughed again.

"Not great things, actually." Mauricio laughed too and realized that it felt good to be able to share a laugh in such carefree way.

"I heard them talking about me when they didn't realize I was there. I heard 'stupid brat' and 'spoiled breed.' I'm sure that they were being polite," Rosie said with levity.

"No, that's pretty much about it. What I heard was more or less along the same line."

"I feel better, already."

"Why are you here?" He knew it all too well now, but it felt the right thing to ask.

"I wanted a baby," Rosie said with a clipped voice.

"Is your wife here with you?"

"No." Rosie's voice had become very cold.

Mauricio felt a weight on his chest at her answer. "I didn't mean to pry."

Rosie stared at a corner for few seconds, breathed slow and then finally looked at him again. "You didn't. Your question was to be expected," she said in a gentler tone.

Mauricio thought that, if anything, his question wasn't to be expected at all, him being a slave and she, the President's daughter.

"I'm not married. I'm here by myself," she admitted slowly.

Mauricio sensed there was something else she wasn't saying, but he wasn't going to make the same mistake twice.

Rosie decided to satiate his curiosity anyway. "I don't want to do the things that are expected of me," she said with a timid smile.

"Don't tell me," Mauricio couldn't help to reply.

"I'm sorry... I seem to be very clumsy with words around you. It's that I've never talked to a slave before." Rosie realized that she had just done it again and put a hand over her mouth. "It's just that I don't know what to say..."

"It's okay. I feel the same way, but I like that you talk to me." Mauricio felt like he was in a dreamlike state again. It happened a lot where Rosie was concerned.

"I do, too. I don't act with you. I don't have to put on a mask. I smile because I want to," Rosie said, as if she was realizing it at that moment. "It is so refreshing to be able to just be myself. Not the President's daughter everybody has to like in public, not the spoiled brat nobody likes in private. Just Rosie." She paused for a moment and then added, "But I'm afraid I don't even know how to be just Rosie. Because I've never been just me. I've never been good enough for the rest of the world."

Rosie looked back at Mauricio and started laughing. "Poor me, right? I'm complaining about my life to a slave!" she said between chuckles. "Oops... I guess that I'm beyond salvation at this point." Rosie tried to stop laughing, but any attempt failed and she doubled over, unable to sober up.

"I'm not offended. I *am* a slave." Mauricio shrugged his shoulders.

"I know, and it's not funny."

"No, it's not. Not for me at least," he said with a gentle tone.

"I know!"

Mauricio heard the machine at his right beeping softly, he turned around and saw that the there was no liquid dripping from the bag to the pipe connected to his arm. He shot a warning look at Rosie one second before a nurse came into the room.

"Mistress! What are you doing here?" The nurse, a middle-aged woman with a graceless voice, looked wildly around, trying to assess what she was seeing.

"Did he attack you?" the nurse asked, worried.

"This slave is bound to a bed with an IV attached to his arm. I bet he can barely walk. How could he attack me?" Rosie had changed tone completely.

Mauricio saw the transformation before his eyes and couldn't believe she was the same person he had been talking to. The girl staring down at the nurse was haughty and cold. Rosie almost looked like a younger version of the Priestess.

"These rooms are all the same. I'm late for my check," she said as if it was the nurse's fault.

"Oh, I'm sorry. You're right, of course, Mistress. The hallway of the birth center isn't, well—" The nurse was interrupted by a single stare from Rosie. "If you want to follow me, I'll escort you to your room."

"Let's go." Rosie walked out with her back straight. The nurse scampered outside with a worried expression on her face.

Please, please, look at me, just one more time… It had pained him to see that she could be like the other women. It shouldn't have been a surprise, and yet it was. He thought about her the whole day. And, when he wasn't thinking about her, he played in his mind, over and over again, the Priestess' words. Not that he had anything else to do, in any case. The doctor came later on to take a look at his vitals, but she didn't seem greatly concerned. Mauricio knew that the Priestess' interest in his wellbeing had actually given him angrier enemies, if that was even possible given his status as untouchable, among both men and women.

He wasn't an ordinary semental slave anymore. He was now the semental slave guards were losing their job over. Not a nice position to be in. The doctor was looking at him, and Mauricio shivered in anticipation of what was coming.

"I know why the Priestess wants you alive and well, but I don't like it. You better behave, or... else," the doctor said.

Mauricio knew all too well what 'else' meant. He lowered his head in submission and didn't complain when the doctor yanked the needle out of his arm. Had he complained, the doctor would have found some new, painful analysis he needed. As it was, she grumbled something and then called two guards to take the slave back to his cell.

He walked between the two guards, almost grateful that he was going back to the familiarity of his cell. While passing by one of the doors opening into the hallway, he heard Rosie's voice. Without warning, the guard in front of him slowed down and he collided into her.

"Don't touch me." The guard pushed him out of the way.

He staggered, lost his footing and ended on the floor. "Get up, you idiot," the second guard said.

Give me a moment, for Heavens' sake.

The women must have heard the Priestess' voice because they stopped for a moment to listen; the door was open and a shaft of light flooded the darkness. Mauricio raised his head and saw Rosie deep in conversation with the Priestess. The older woman was wearing a plain green gown over her usual garish dress and she was reading something from a tablet. Rosie was lying on a bed, her body covered by white linen. He saw her absentmindedly wrapping her fingers around a corner of the linen sheet.

"The baby is fine. She survived the worst. In a week or two, if everything keeps improving, and I don't see why it wouldn't, you are going home for good." The Priestess' tone was calm, but it was clear that she had been repeating the same words several times.

"After all the blood I lost last time, I'm still worried that my baby isn't going to make it," Rosie said.

"Yes, I admit I would be scared too, but you are young, and the baby is strong. She's going to have a wonderful life." The Priestess talked to Rosie with a mix of sympathy and irritation.

"I know you don't want me here. I'll be out of the way as soon as you can assure me that my baby is one hundred percent fine," Rosie said matter-of-factly.

"It's not—" The Priestess shook her head.

"I don't care if you like me or not. I probably wouldn't like me if I were in your place. The only thing that matters is the health of my baby. I know that you wouldn't send me home just to get rid of me. I trust your integrity on this." Rosie's words were out of line, even for the President's daughter.

Mauricio's guards gasped loudly, and all of a sudden, both the Priestess and Rosie turned around and saw them. Rosie's eyes locked with Mauricio's for a brief moment and then she turned around again to face anything but him. But Mauricio saw *her*.

"What are you doing out there?" the Priestess asked, cross from the interruption. She closed the door with a slam without waiting for an answer.

"On our way to his cell," one of the two guards answered anyway. She pulled Mauricio up and against the wall and murmured to him, "Walk." She didn't have to add any menacing words to it; the tone said it all.

Soon after, he was left in his cell, the fourth or fifth—he had lost track—of the six promised meals arrived and he ate. Mauricio spent what little was left of the day nibbling at his food and napping. Soon, darkness engulfed his cell and Mauricio waited to hear her steps. Although he tried to keep his eyes opened and his mind alert, he was still weak and dozed on and off. At one point in the evening, he rested his head on the bed and stared at the window.

"Are you there?" Rosie's voice came from the outside world, bringing with her a playful gust of air.

Mauricio sat up immediately and stretched his sleepy body.

"Yes," he answered back.

"How are you now?" she asked. Her voice sounded closer to Mauricio's cell.

"Much better, thanks." Mauricio felt even better now.

"I had to cut you dead today," she said softly.

"I understood." Mauricio didn't say that it had really stung.

"I didn't want you to be in any trouble," she explained in the same tone.

"I know." It was good to hear it out loud. "But... you sounded so different..."

"Like the spoiled brat everybody talks about?"

He didn't confirm her words, but his lips curved up.

"It's okay; I know I can be obnoxious. I'm really good at that. It's one of my favorite characters. The spoiled brat keeps the brownnosers away." Rosie chuckled her crystalline laugh.

"I imagine she has been useful to you."

"You have no idea how hard it is to mete between the people I can trust and the ones who only want to take advantage of me." Rosie wasn't laughing anymore; her voice had grown serious in a matter of seconds.

"No, I don't." Mauricio was somber. He was frustrated by the fact that even using the same alphabet, they were speaking two different languages. Their lives were opposing to the point that even the same word didn't mean the same thing for either of them. "I am alone. And I'm normally at the receiving end of the *meting out*." His dad had used to tell him religious stories and the verb 'mete' was associated in Mauricio's memory with ancient tales of justice and retribution. His dad had told him beautiful stories of a time when the men weren't slaves. Now, as a man, Mauricio thought that probably his dad had invented the tales for him.

"Sometimes I wish I wasn't so alone. It's painful," Mauricio said to the wall.

"Sometimes I wish I had the power to change the things I don't like," Rosie continued.

"Like what? You're a woman; you can do anything you want! What would you like to change so much?" Mauricio asked, interested.

"The fact that you're a slave," Rosie simply answered.

Once again, Mauricio was speechless.

"I don't think it's right."

"I agree," Mauricio managed to say. Something deep inside him broke at her words. "I don't think your mother is going to be happy to hear that, though," he said after having steadied his voice. He sounded almost cheerful.

"No, she isn't proud of me. I'm the daughter her publicist had suggested to hide in some forgotten college. I came here to have a child out of wedlock instead," Rosie said in a light tone, but her pause at the end said otherwise.

"Do they know that you are here?"

"No. I've managed the impossible. I've tricked the whole Presidential staff, my two lovely mothers, and their less-than-lovely publicist into thinking that I was going to do what they had suggested. Everybody back home thinks I am studying marine biology in a remote college." She laughed heartily.

"How did you do that?" Mauricio asked to keep the conversation going. He wasn't ready to talk at length, yet.

"I bribed lots and lots of people. And my mothers are paying for my tuition.'" Rosie sounded satisfied and Mauricio smiled at the tone of her voice.

"You know another thing I would change if I could?" Rosie asked abruptly.

"No, what is it?" Mauricio was amazed that a woman with so many privileges had unfulfilled desires.

"I would love to raise this baby by myself. Alone. Somewhere far away from Ginecea and the Presidential Palace."

"What will happen to you if your mothers find out?" Mauricio couldn't imagine that the President's daughter could escape her heritage easily.

"*When* they find me, which I know is just a matter of time—I am not delusional—I'll be stored away somewhere I can't create a scandal. The family publicist is going to find a solution to the problem," Rosie said the last words with a broken voice. "I'm just biding my time to give my baby a chance," she added as an afterthought.

"I heard what the Priestess was telling you..." Mauricio didn't know if she wanted to talk about it.

"I almost lost my baby and I was so worried about her; she is so tiny and I couldn't do anything to help her."

"But your baby is fine now," Mauricio repeated the Priestess' words. He sensed something stirring inside when talking about this baby Rosie was carrying. There was this tingling in his stomach and the odd happiness that he couldn't help feeling. *Our baby...* he thought. *I know this is blasphemous, but this baby could be mine... Actually, I'm almost sure she's mine.* The more he thought about it, the more all the half-conversations he had accidentally heard led to that conclusion, even though Mauricio was well aware that it went against the core of beliefs on which the Ginecean society was built. *I'm still alive after I was caught in Rosie's room, and the Priestess ordered I'm not to be touched in case they still need my semen. Why else could it be?*

"Yes, she's a strong one." Rosie's voice was happier now.

"She's going to be fine," Mauricio said again. He had a sudden desire to hug Rosie. He imagined her small body in the cradle of his embrace. It felt right.

"I like it," Rosie said, taking him by surprise.

"What?" *Can you read my mind?* Mauricio thought.

"I like the way you said it, that my baby is going to be fine. You sounded so sure of it, as if you know. It makes me feel better."

Mauricio was pleased by her statement and the longing to be in her presence became stronger. "You know what I'd like to change at this precise moment?"

"No, what would you?" Rosie's voice came labored, as if she was pacing back and forth. Steps were resonating outside.

"I'd like to tear down this wall in front of me."

"Why?" she asked after a second.

"I want to hold you," Mauricio said without hesitating. A silence louder than one thousand voices echoed inside the cell and Mauricio shivered. He slowly slid from the bed to the floor and threw his head back. He sat, staring at the dark ceiling, waiting for her to say something. When it was painfully clear that Rosie wasn't going to say anything, Mauricio slapped his head with both hands and then pressed them against his temples to mitigate the oncoming headache. Then he heard steps coming closer.

"Mistress! What are you doing out here, alone?" It was a young woman's voice.

"Hi, nurse Celia. I like to come here at night and sing to my baby. The eucalyptus tree keeps me company and the view of the lake is too beautiful to miss." Rosie's voice was subdued and not at all haughty.

Mauricio wondered why she was being nice to the nurse.

"Don't worry; I won't tell the Priestess that you leave your room at night. But you have to promise me to be careful. Don't do anything stupid to compromise the health of your baby girl," Nurse Celia said.

"I would never do anything to harm her. You know that. She is the only thing in the world I care for," Rosie said, lowering her voice.

"You are going to be a wonderful mother."

For several minutes, neither the nurse nor Rosie said anything and Mauricio imagined that they were contemplating the view he would never see. He stared at the wall instead, waiting for the nurse to leave. He wanted to talk to Rosie, to apologize to her. He knew he had spoken out of line.

"Mistress Rosie, I will accompany you back to your room. It's very late and it's starting to rain," Nurse Celia said with a tone that didn't allow cajoling from Rosie.

"I guess that's all for tonight then, my dear friend." Rosie had come closer to Mauricio's wall. Her voice resonated loud and clear through the window's bars.

"You really like this tree, don't you?" Nurse Celia asked with an amused laugh.

"I do," Rosie answered immediately.

Mauricio heard the steps growing softer and was left with the urge to bang his head against the wall. He was happy. And completely exhausted. He climbed back on the bed, hugged the rough linen of his sheet, and fell asleep immediately. He dreamed of Rosie and of a young girl with Rosie's features and his colors. The girl, three or four years old, was the most beautiful thing he had ever seen, and he knew he loved her.

CHAPTER 6

Mauricio woke up the next morning to the sound of chirping birds, which he now knew lived on the eucalyptus tree just outside his cell. The rest of the world was so close to him, yet still miles away. But his happiness from the night before lingered, and the sad consideration didn't change his mood. Rosie had called him 'dear friend.' She hadn't been offended by his words. He felt energized.

When the new guard came, he wasn't surprised to see a different woman banging good morning on the bars of his cell. He thought that as women went, this one wasn't terribly mean. For example, she banged only twice instead of the usual half a dozen attempts to destroy his ears. Although he couldn't find anything else decent about the guard, he decided it was enough. Mauricio was surprised that, instead of taking him directly to the deposit room as usual, she opened a door that led to a place he had heard about, but had never seen. He was even more surprised when the guard ordered him inside.

"You have ten minutes to eat," the guard said.

He had never seen so much food, and his stomach started rumbling at the sight. He couldn't believe he had been admitted inside a dining room. And he was completely alone. He ate until he felt his stomach would burst, and he still had time to waste. The idea that maybe he should have been worried by the unexpected boon passed through his mind, but he was full for the first time in his life and yet he decided to reach for another helping.

"Time's up," the guard announced from the doorway. Mauricio couldn't eat anything else, anyway. He grabbed a few pieces of bread while passing the table and stuffed them in his pockets, which he realized the guard caught him doing, but she turned her head away. He started worrying.

"The doctor will take a look at you now," the guard said, without the customary sneer. Mauricio went through the door she had opened for him and braced himself for the worst.

"Remove everything and wear this gown," the doctor ordered Mauricio. He went to the corner behind a screen and did as instructed. He felt a distinct sense of déjà vu. He was subjected to the same treatment he received four years earlier, down to the cold fingers probing him in an uncomfortable way. Even the request at the end was the same.

"Fill the cup," the doctor said.

Mauricio went behind the screen and did his best not to disappoint the doctor. Somehow he knew that if she wasn't happy with the result, his day was going to change drastically. He closed his eyes and tried to forget that on the other side of the thin layer of rice paper, the doctor waited. He breathed slowly in and out, and the image of Rosie appeared behind his eyelids. Mauricio's mind slowly relaxed and his body followed.

"Done?" The doctor tapped on the screen's frame.

Mauricio closed the lid tightly on the cup and put it on the window-tray at his side. The doctor heard the click of the tray receding inside the window and told him to wait where he was. He remained seated to contemplate the white wall before him. Mauricio was good at waiting; he had done it all his life. Normally, he just let his mind wander between thoughts. It was his way to escape from his imprisonment. But this time, something was off. The meal he had stuffed into his hungry stomach was a sign of something he couldn't fathom; the doctor personally supervising his production was another clue of a larger picture he wasn't seeing.

"Well, at least you are good for something," the doctor commented.

Someone entered the room. Mauricio peeked through the frame of the screen and saw his new guard walking toward his corner. Shortly after, the imposing figure of the Priestess filled the space, and the doctor bowed to her. He sat down.

"We finally have enough to freeze. The semen is in perfect condition, despite the treatment the semental received during the last month," the doctor said.

"Thank the Heavens I came back in time to supervise the whole procedure," the Priestess commented and then added, "We are done with him."

The guard moved the screen, one hand already on the whip.

"It will never happen again," the Priestess said under her breath when her eyes found Mauricio, sitting on the chair. He shivered at the tone of her voice.

The guard sensed his hesitation and tugged him by his sleeve. He moved along but gave a last look at the Priestess. She looked back at him with disgust. He walked, knowing exactly what was going to happen. He wasn't useful anymore. His days as a semental were over. He was going to be employed in the fields. Finally, he was going to see the sun. Finally, he was going to have a place among the other slaves. This should have been the happiest day of his miserable life, but he could only think that he would never hear Rosie's voice again.

He knew that she was going to leave him soon anyway, but he thought that he still had some time to spend talking to her from the safe haven of his cell. Now, it was all too sudden. He followed the guard back to his cell, putting one foot in front of the other automatically, so it came as another unpleasant surprise when he realized that he was somewhere else entirely.

"Get in," the guard commanded him with a gun aimed at his head.

Mauricio thought that it was uncalled for since the collar on his neck was already stinging painfully, and he wasn't even tugging at it. He climbed two steps and found himself inside a small room, about the size of his cell, with two rows of seats facing each other. There were two more men sitting down, strapped to the seats and firmly shackled to the floor. His guard pushed him into the first free spot and briskly anchored Mauricio on the seat like the other two slaves. From the painful expression on their faces, their collars were giving them hell, too. A metallic shutter rolled down and walled the space where the bars usually were.

The room was humming. Mauricio felt the roar vibrating under his feet and spreading though his body. The guard sat on the opposite row facing the three slaves. She, too, strapped her body to the seat. The roar became louder and the seats moved. Or, was it that the whole room moved with the seats? Mauricio didn't have time to speculate further about what was happening because the most excruciating pain exploded in his neck and traveled up to the roots of his hair and down to his toes. He couldn't help but scream as the pain spread to his teeth.

"Shut the collars off!" the guard yelled and banged on the wall. A metallic sound resonated in the room. She repeated the order twice and kept banging on the wall until someone from the other side shouted back.

Mauricio noticed that the pain was gone, but his brain wasn't responding to outside stimuli. He kept twitching.

"I thought you had shut them off already!" A window on the wall opened, or more precisely, a section of the wall went down, and the face of a woman bathed in a bright glow appeared. Mauricio's eyes were offended by the sudden luminosity and he shut them tight.

"No. That was your job, not mine," the guard answered. "You better hope that these slaves didn't suffer permanent damage. The manager at Tarin is going to demote you as soon as she finds out," she added, almost gleefully.

"Why should she? Nothing happened. It was just an oversight. Nobody died," the woman behind the window replied, ignoring the tone of the other.

"Tarin's manager doesn't like damaged goods," the guard kept pressing the subject.

Mauricio hoped that they would stop talking. He was still in a considerable amount of pain, and the room was moving, making him even more uncomfortable.

"They're still in one piece," the sitting woman proclaimed with a shrug and disappeared behind the opening.

Mauricio felt the urge to throw up. His stomach heaved and he couldn't do anything to stop it. In a matter of seconds, the food he had eaten with such abandon was cast on the floor. The man closer to Mauricio cringed and tried to move his shackled leg away from him. The guard, whose boots had been soiled by his breakfast binge, howled in fury.

"Great! That's the last thing I need today, a carsick slave." She slammed her right hand on the wall behind her. "Stop the van. I need to open the door for few minutes to let some fresh air in."

At her words, the roar ceased and the room stopped moving. Mauricio raised his head and turned around in time to see the guard standing up and pushing a button next to the metallic shutter.

"Much better," she murmured under her breath when the wall rolled up with a clattering sound and the room was filled with bright light and crisp air.

Mauricio wasn't sure what he was looking at, exactly. The quality of the light and the scent in the air were completely different from what he was used to. When his eyes finally focused beyond the brightness, Mauricio gasped and, at the same time, the guard pushed him out. He hit the ground, his feet fumbling in the air and his hands barely breaking the fall. The rich flavor of dry dirt filled his mouth, tickled his nose, and made him sneeze.

"I'm going to unlock your hands, so you can clean yourself up. Don't try anything, or you'll regret it." The guard came closer, waving a key in her left hand while her right was ready on the holster, showing him what her intentions were regarding punishment.

I'm outside… I'm outside… I'm really outside. I can't believe it. Since birth, Mauricio had spent all his life inside, moved from one wing of the facility to another. He had dreamed of this moment and recently, thanks to the window in his cell, he had even had a limited experience of what lay outside, which, in turn, had led him to fantasize even more about seeing the world outside his cell. But he had never expected that actually seeing the outside with his eyes was going to be so intense as to leave him incapable of following the guard's order. *I'm going to faint again. This, this air, is making me lightheaded. I like it. It's so bright out here, so many colors. What's that?* His head snapped to follow every little change in the scenery. Something moved on his far right, but it was too far away and too fast; a gust of wind transported small, light-green leaves from a nearby tree to his feet, but they were gone already by the time he thought of catching one in his hands. *Come back here.*

He almost didn't hear the woman yelling at him to get going, nor he did he seem to realize that she had thrown a rag that hit him in the face. His legs were trembling, but he felt better than he had ever felt. He bent to pick up the rag and acting out of sheer habit, he cleaned himself. All of his senses were focused on basking in the sunlight and breathing in the air that smelled of the flowers and trees he had never seen. *This is what outside looks like.* A smile appeared on his face before he could hide his joy from the guard.

"What's up with you? The electricity fried your brain?" the woman asked under her breath.

"We have to move, otherwise we'll never reach Tarin before tonight," the guard behind the wall called with an annoyed tone.

Please, please let me stay here. Mauricio's eyes filled with angry tears. Another fast-running dot crossed the field. *I'll never know what that is.*

"Almost done here. Don't complain; it's your fault for not having shut off the collars before leaving the Temple."

"Your fault, you mean. I drive; you take care of the slaves."

Please, I'm not done yet. I haven't had enough time outside. I need more. I need to know what those things are that are running so fast.

"Whatever." The guard, satisfied by Mauricio's cleaning, tied his hands together, nudged her gun against his shoulder blades, commanded him to get inside the van, and pushed the button to roll down the shutter again.

Once the fresh air was replaced by the aroma of the human bodies, Mauricio moaned loudly. *I'm going to suffocate; this place, it's too small. I can't breathe.*

"Don't get sick on me again, or I'll forget that Tarin is waiting for three slaves," the guard menaced, but Mauricio wasn't listening to her anymore.

The trip from the Temple to Tarin took the whole day. Mauricio and the other two men were allowed to relieve themselves twice. When the guard stopped the van to take a break, Mauricio couldn't believe that she was going to let him out again.

I am out. He wanted to laugh and cry at the same time. Overloads of contrasting emotions were fighting to dominate one another. Laughing won. He put his feet down gingerly, as if by touching the red soil, it would shatter and disappear. *I wonder what it feels like to walk with my bare feet on it.* He looked around to see if the women were checking on him.

"You, do what you're supposed to," the driver warned him, whip in hand.

I hate you. Mauricio sighed and limited himself to getting down on his knees and scooping some red dirt in his hands. *It disappears between my fingers, like water, but it's different.* He looked at his hands, colored by the remaining dust, and brought them closer to his nose. *Oh...* He sneezed before finishing his thought. A melodic noise echoed in the crisp air and he raised his head to follow a small, dark-blue and brown body flying toward a tree. The elation he had felt a moment earlier was replaced by an emotion that left him looking for air. "A bird singing... this is what a bird looks like. I've never thought that something so small could produce such sounds." His eyes filled with tears. Something else caught his attention. *What are you? A bug?* He crouched to take a closer look at a blade of grass that was arched down by something black and round. A whole symphony of chirping and clicking started a few seconds later and he smiled in recognition. *Yes, you and your friends sound like the bugs outside my cell.*

"How long do we have to stay here?" the driver asked, already climbing inside the van.

"Inside, now," the guard ordered. "What's so funny, idiot?" She gave Mauricio a sharp look.

He waited a moment longer outside, and when she turned to insult the other men, he grabbed a fallen leaf from the ground and put it in his pocket.

The third time the van stopped, it was late in the afternoon and the sun was a golden disk hovering in the sky.

This is a sunset. No wonder the field workers talk so much about it. Mauricio stared at the sight, eyes bright and mouth dangling open. "Have you ever seen anything like that before?" he asked the two men squatting behind a short bush. They looked at each other and then back at him as if he was mad. "Look at the colors! Did you know that the reds and the yellows could mix together? And the blue of the sky… Look how it's changing before our eyes," he continued, incapable of stopping. He needed to share his emotions with someone else. *Rosie, I wish you were here with me, under this sky bleeding red and orange and yellow.*

"Idiot, stop talking; you aren't here to make conversation," the guard reminded him.

Without warning, the whip made contact with his back and he fell on all fours to the ground. He felt hard objects under his hands and knees and when he lifted himself, he noticed that he had landed on a sea of multicolored pebbles.

"Time to go," the driver called.

He collected one of the pebbles and looked as it changed colors when moved this way and that under the sunlight.

"Are you deaf?" the guard asked him.

Mauricio quickly hid the pebble in his closed hand and took one final breath. The wind played with the brunches of a tall, weeping tree and a balmy scent penetrated inside his nose and opened his lungs. He breathed slowly and let the fragrance fill him, leaving him clean and refreshed. When he was back inside the stuffy passenger compartment of the van, he closed his eyes and touched the pebble and the leaf, imagining that he was still out there with the birds and the bugs.

Several hours later, when Mauricio's body had reached its limit, the guard announced their arrival. The van stopped and she went to open the shutter. It was dark outside, but Mauricio could make out the silhouette of a building. It was big and tall and towered over the short vegetation surrounding the place. He looked at it forebodingly. Mauricio hoped the guard would let him find the privacy of a bush before doing anything else. Apparently, letting the slaves use the latrine wasn't high on the list of the guard's priorities any longer.

"You're officially out of my hair now," she said, clearly relieved when a tall door opened, revealing a light inside the building. She saw another guard walking briskly toward them and went to meet her. The two women exchanged greetings that betrayed the fact that they were more than simply acquainted and then remembered, several minutes later, that there was human cargo to take care of.

The inside of the building wasn't as majestic as the outside. The guards walked them past two hallways, then down a flight of stairs that ended at a large chamber lit by sconces. There, Mauricio and the two slaves were separated. The two men were taken into custody by the new guard, and Mauricio was led just outside the chamber and left to wait in a small room with a disproportionately tall ceiling and four circular holes at shoulder's height. The room was drafty as a result of the small windows, but Mauricio didn't mind the cold. It kept him sharp after so many hours of dozing on and off. It also helped that the room had a small toilet hidden behind a screen. After having relieved himself, Mauricio sat on the floor and started playing with his two new treasures; he rolled the pebble with his fingers and gently traced the contours of the leaf. After a while, it became clear that nobody was coming for him. This room was his new cell. He took a better look at it and he didn't like what he saw. The draft wasn't pleasant anymore. Mauricio was cold and hungry by the time someone remembered that he was there.

MONICA LA PORTA

CHAPTER 7

"Let's get to work." A guard came to pick him up.

At least this one is happy, Mauricio thought. In twenty-two years, he had been passed around by so many guards that he couldn't recognize one face from the other. But this one was different; she looked happy.

"Have you ever worked in the fields?" the guard asked.

Mauricio turned his head sideways, looking for the person she was talking to.

"So, have you?" the guard, who didn't look old, but had a long white braid that contrasted with her dark eyes, asked again.

Mauricio turned his head one more time, but the guard's gaze didn't go past him.

"Do you still have your tongue?"

Mauricio had to admit that she wasn't hideous, and that she hadn't touched him yet, although she was sporting a whip and a gun, just like every other guard he had met.

"I've never worked in the fields," he said, looking nervously at the woman. He hoped that she wasn't the type who got a kick out of getting slaves in trouble. He had met *that* guard before many times. It hadn't been pleasant at all.

"You were a semental, right?" she asked, looking at him now.

Mauricio felt her eyes on him and didn't know what to think. Guards normally didn't look directly at slaves or talk to them. "Yes." He thought it better to keep his answer simple.

"You've never been outside then," she stated. "It's hard work outside, but you'll probably like the change of venue." The guard showed him the way.

Mauricio felt confused by the sad look she gave him after the last sentence. He didn't know if he was supposed to reply to her words or not. So he decided to wait and see what was required of him.

"Who gave you your name? Mauricio is a unique name for a slave," the guard asked, still looking at him.

How do you know my name? And why do you care? "My father gave me this name when I was five or six." Mauricio found that he wasn't comfortable with the guard's eyes focused on him. He wasn't used to it. It completely ruined all his efforts of being inconspicuous.

"You can call me Guen, by the way." The guard smiled at him.

What did she just say? Mauricio couldn't be more surprised by the last bit of conversation. *There is something completely wrong about this. A guard is talking to me, asking personal questions. Maybe I'm still sleeping.* His level of uneasiness was rapidly growing uncomfortable. *I hope she leaves me alone.* He focused on the act of walking. She didn't say anything else, and Mauricio had the time to look at his surroundings. They remained on the same floor, which was one lower than the entry level. *I don't like it here. This place is scarier in the light of day than it was last night. The ceiling is too high, the tiled floor radiates cold, and the draft is chilling my bones.* He followed the woman from one side of the building to the other in blessed silence. *This hallway goes forever and it's so dark without windows.* Finally, Guen slowed down and stopped before a big door with an equally big window at its center that let in white light. *Heavens bless me; it looks bright out there.* Mauricio peeked at the view, but he had to avert his eyes for a moment.

"Here we are. Let me recalibrate your collar first so that you can get out, and then I'll leave you in the capable hands of your field boss. See you later tonight." A moment later, Guen made a small gesture of salute with one hand to her head, opened the door for him, held it until he walked through and then turned away.

Mauricio was too shocked to say anything at all and couldn't shrug the feeling that there was something ominous going on. He rubbed his eyes at the onslaught of natural light.

"I know, it's hard to get used to the fact that there are nice women," a male voice intruded on Mauricio's thoughts. He turned to his right and was face-to-face with a slave whose age he couldn't tell. The man was taller than Mauricio, strongly built, with olive skin and dark hair sprinkled with silver. His eyes were the most distinctive feature of his whole face: steel gray, speckled with green.

"I'm Arias, your field boss. Welcome to Tarin." The man offered Mauricio his outstretched hand and a warm smile.

"I'm Mauricio." He held the other man's hand reluctantly, intimidated by his field boss.

"Follow me to the cafeteria where you can have something to eat and drink," Arias said while walking toward a low building on their right. "By the way, your collar is on another frequency, but it still works outside. And, I can assure you first hand, it stings." The man's hand went automatically to his collar.

"I know, 'Don't do anything stupid or else.' Don't worry; I'm not the kind of person who does stupid things." Mauricio waved his hand in the air. He was frustrated and his tone reflected his sentiment.

"I wasn't worried," Arias said, seemingly amused by Mauricio's outburst.

"I didn't sleep, and I didn't eat. My new accommodation is cold and drafty. The guard who escorted me here, Guen, is nice to me."

"I already told you. It takes some time to adjust to Guen." Arias was laughing with mirth. "Regarding the lack of sleep, you will just have to resist until tonight, but at least you get to eat now."

"Can you do anything about the cell?" Mauricio asked, repressing a smile.

"No, unfortunately, I have no jurisdiction on the accommodations. I can make your life easier while you are here, though." Arias gave a sideways look at Mauricio. They had reached their destination.

"While I am here? I am not supposed to stay here until I die?" Mauricio had heard the slight change of tone when Arias had said it.

"That is what I meant," Arias answered, holding the door open for Mauricio. Inside the cafeteria, there were other men, and it took some time to introduce Mauricio to the others.

"Is it always like this?" Mauricio asked, after he had already eaten more than his usual share of food.

"More or less." Arias took a sip from his steaming cup.

"What's that you're drinking?" Mauricio asked, smelling the strong aroma.

"Coffee. Would you like some?"

"I don't know. I've never had anything but water." Mauricio wiggled his nose inhaling the robust scent wafting his way.

"We can make things right immediately. I'll fetch a cup for you." Arias stood up and went to the table with all the assorted beverages.

Mauricio looked around, relaxing in his chair. He wasn't used to any of this, but he could get comfortable, eventually. He nibbled on the last piece of bread left on his plate and thought of how his life was changing. He noticed that Arias had found someone on his way back and was talking animatedly. Mauricio looked at the scene with envy. No man had ever talked to him that way, with the exception of his father. And Rosie, who liked to spend time with him, even though he wasn't a woman. He missed her.

"Hey, you!" Someone tapped Mauricio's shoulder.

"Yes?" He turned around to face three men who were looking back at him with curious faces. They were balancing generous portions of food on their trays.

"Is it true that you're from the Temple?" the dark one asked, picking at a piece of bread lying atop another three different layers of meats and vegetables. His big fingers clumsily knocked off a morsel of dark meat that fell out of the tray and landed on the floor. The man didn't seem to notice.

What a waste. "Yes." Mauricio wasn't used to conversation and also wasn't sure that he wanted to talk to them. These three men didn't look friendly.

"Say, are you one of *them*?" the one with lighter skin and a mustache asked, accentuating the last word with a sneer. "You don't mind, do you?" He sat at Mauricio's table and then motioned for the other men to join him.

I do mind. "One of whom?" Mauricio was already regretting having turned around.

"You have the clean face of a semental. Yes, you definitely do," the third one, a short guy with frizzy, red hair, said, playing with his fork and sending rice everywhere.

Mauricio calmly cleared his tray of the stray food that had landed on it.

"We could help with that, though," the dark one said.

"Yes, we're good friends. We can break your face for you. So you won't look so pretty around here," Mustache added with a smile that made Mauricio cringe.

"Leave him alone." Coming from behind, a fourth man interrupted the series of suggestions about rearranging Mauricio's features. He pulled a chair from a nearby table and sat at Mauricio's.

"Or what?" Red hair was clearly the belligerent type.

"You know exactly *what*," the man answered calmly. He was young and thinly built, but there was something about the way he talked that made an impression on Mauricio. The other three men evidently thought the same because they stood up and left after few rude remarks about sementals and the people who went to the trouble to defend them. They left behind a trail of food on the table.

Wasteful idiots. Mauricio had his eyes on them until they disappeared in the crowd.

"Don't mind them," the man said, crossing his arms on his chest.

"Good morning, Leander." Arias had finally found his way back, although Mauricio had the distinct feeling that the older man had waited on purpose. Leander nodded back.

"Leander, this is Mauricio. Mauricio, this is Leander." Arias put a steaming cup of coffee before Mauricio and mimed the act of drinking. "Try a small sip, and be careful because it's hot," he warned.

"It's... hot *and* bitter," Mauricio said, while pressing his palm against his scorched lip. The other two men laughed.

"Another thing you'll have to get used to," Arias said, sipping his coffee.

"I'm addicted to this stuff," Leander added.

"So, Leander here is going to show you what to do." Arias stood up, and without adding anything else, left.

Mauricio was getting a furious headache. And he was getting anxious. He didn't understand what was happening. He felt comfortable with the three thugs making fun of him, for that was his reality. The atmosphere in the cafeteria was putting him on edge. He looked around and saw men chatting and talking to each other or just readying themselves for a long day of work. They seemed happy, not terrorized by the thought they could be breathing their last air.

"Deep in thought, huh?" Leander put his empty cup down on the table. The sound, more than Leander's words, brought Mauricio back to the present.

"In less than two days my life has changed completely, and I'm not sure what to think," Mauricio cautiously answered.

"I wasn't born here myself. I came to Tarin only a year ago. And, like you, I hadn't had the time of my life." Leander took the cup and went to refill it. Mauricio looked at his new acquaintance and noticed that Leander limped slightly.

"How can you tell?" Mauricio asked when he came back.

"I happen to have a pretty face as well, in case you haven't noticed." Leander raised one of his brows and then smiled.

"You were a semental?" Mauricio was surprised. He took another sip of his lukewarm coffee.

"Yep. I came here straight from the Temple." Leander's eyes were scanning the room.

"You were there?"

"I even saw the Priestess, once." Leander was now focused on a group of men sitting by the entry, at the other end of the room.

"I did, too, recently. More than I wanted, actually." Mauricio found the coincidence interesting.

"We better start our day," Leander announced and turned his head toward the exit.

Mauricio couldn't help but notice the long stares Leander and the group of men exchanged. They weren't friendly, but at the same time, there wasn't any hostility between them. Leander didn't pause to make introductions, so Mauricio followed him outside to the fields.

"You're going to like it. Not immediately, not today for sure, but you'll appreciate the opportunity to work under the sun," Leander said and then turned to face Mauricio. "Enjoy every moment of it," he finished.

They walked, following a path paved in bricks that cut through a sea of tall grass, Mauricio trailing his arms low to touch the tops of the foliage, waving in time with the light breeze. His mind went into overload; the colors his eyes were seeing were too bright; the sky was too blue, and the grass too green. Even though he had experienced the thrill of being outside just the day before, he was conditioned to the dull colors of the inside world of the Temple, where everything was a shade of gray. *I'll never get used to this.* The colors were pure and undiluted, and the light shone bright—even the smells were too intense. *Was it so vivid yesterday?* The grass had a peculiar scent he couldn't define with words, but it was fresh. *The air is so crisp that it's stinging my nose, but the sun is warm on my skin.* His fingers were prickled by the rigid texture of the stems forming the sea of undulating green grass. *"Where are all the bugs?"*

"I remember my first day outside," Leander said, after several minutes of silence.

Mauricio was glad he was given some time to contemplate the scenery. "It's magnificent," he murmured. He hated that his voice betrayed his inner turmoil. He was in awe.

"Yes." Leander nodded and looked away.

Mauricio raised his head toward the sky, closed his eyes and let the sun caress his skin.

"I should've given you a hat," Leander commented. "You are going to be tomato red by the end of today."

"I don't care," Mauricio thought out loud.

"You don't care now," Leander replied softly, but he didn't add anything else to the subject.

"What do we do today?" Mauricio asked with interest.

"You'll help dig a trench, and I'll help remove the soil from the digging."

They had reached the end of the sea of grass, and before them was a vast expanse of brown land covered in rectangles and squares in different shades of yellow, green, and purple. The view stretched to the horizon and Mauricio saw that the fields went on for miles and miles and a blue ribbon cut the land in two. Mauricio squinted against the sun's glare and noticed that beyond the river, the colors of the fields changed to a palette of oranges, reds, and greens.

"At Tarin, we take care of this side of the field. The other farms are responsible for the orchards on the other side of the river," Leander explained.

"What does Tarin produce?" Mauricio was filling his eyes with the peaceful sight.

"We provide the raw ingredients for cosmetic products. The yellow is our mimosa tree production. The green is made up of several aromatic herbs like sage, lemongrass, rosemary, mint, and thyme. The purple is lavender of thirty different varieties. Tarin got the perfumed bunch." Leander indicated each different square or rectangle with his outstretched hand.

"Where is the trench?" Mauricio asked, since he didn't see anybody digging anything in the vicinity.

"By the river." Leander pointed a finger toward a speck of activity happening far away from them.

"It is going to take the whole day just to reach them!" Mauricio liked the idea of walking, but doubted that it was productive.

"We are waiting for our ride." Leander aimed at another dark speck moving through the fields.

The car, very similar to the van that had brought Mauricio to Tarin, reached them in less than a minute. This time, Mauricio knew what was going to happen and his stomach didn't put up a fight. The field workers' van had windows on both sides, and Mauricio stuck his nose to one and looked outside the entire ride.

When the van stopped to let them out, he was surprised that they had already arrived at their destination. It had looked so far away from the trail.

"I'll introduce you to the digging crew now." Leander accompanied Mauricio toward a group of men intent on excavating a large amount of soil from a big, rectangular hole in the ground.

Mauricio could hear the men joking about something he didn't understand, and he would have stepped back if Leander wasn't already there, pushing him forward.

"Guys, this is Mauricio. Mauricio, these are your mates." Leander smiled at Mauricio and then left to reach his crew.

"Hey!" Mauricio called after Leander, who paused and turned around.

"Do you need anything?" Leander asked with a frown.

"Thanks, for earlier."

"Sure." Leander shrugged his shoulders and walked away.

Mauricio jumped inside the hole to meet his crew. He was greeted by several voices talking all at the same time.

"I'm your boss here. I'm Grey; now take the shovel and start helping." The loudest of the lot threw him a tool and attacked the soil with his own to show Mauricio what was expected from him.

"Nice to meet you. All of you," he said, turning his head right and left to encompass the whole crew of scruffy-looking men with his greeting.

"Likewise," the closest to him answered with a toothless smile.

"See if you are equally happy tonight when we're done," another said and laughed. But it wasn't an unpleasant laugh. It wasn't the scornful laugh that was the guards' trademark.

Mauricio grabbed the shovel with two hands. *It's heavy!* Then he took a good look at what the other men were doing and tried to imitate them. *And it isn't as simple as they make it look.* It took him several minutes to catch up with the others, but Mauricio was satisfied with the result when he started digging in time with the song the crew was singing. *Did they just say... that? I can't believe they said that out loud.* He was so surprised by the double entendres and the overall boldness of the lyrics that he forgot what he was doing.

"Are you okay?" one of the men asked, his eyes pointing at Mauricio's hand.

"Just having fun listening to your songs. Why?" *Am I doing something wrong?* he thought at first, but then looked down, following the other man's gaze, and saw what had prompted the question. "Oh... crap," he said, cradling his bleeding hand. "I don't know how this happened."

"The shovel handle." The man showed him the tool Mauricio had thrown on the ground at the sight of his blood.

"Right—"

Grey came close to Mauricio and gave a perfunctory check at the injured part. "You'll toughen up; don't worry. In a week, tops, you'll have hard calluses to protect your soft skin. You'll look like the rest of us in no time." He then took a handful of green grass from the patch stretching out at the excavation's edge. "Chew the mint and then apply it on your hand. The day past tomorrow, you won't remember you cut yourself."

Mauricio took the handful of what Grey had called mint and chewed on it, as asked. He liked the taste of the mint; it cleansed his mouth, and the smell of the chewed mush went through his nose and straight to his lungs. He gingerly put the mint on the cut skin of his hand. At first, he felt a pang of pain, but after a moment, he felt better.

"It works every time," Grey commented proudly.

"Thanks," Mauricio said while turning the hand sideways, still trying to keep the chewed mint on it.

"Now, back to work. If you can't hold the shovel—"

"No, I'm fine. I can work. I promise." *Heavens forbid I get introduced to another living soul today...* Trying to remember all the names was becoming increasingly harder. *I never thought to admit something like this... but I just discovered I don't dislike being alone that much.* Maybe he was already too old to get acquainted with humanity.

"Okay, but you can't slack; otherwise, I'll have to ask Arias to get you reassigned somewhere else."

"I won't give you any reason to consult Arias on my behalf." Mauricio tried his best formal speech, and it worked. Grey didn't threaten him a second time and let him work with his crew for the whole shift.

When, at the end of the day, the van came back to pick him up, Mauricio could barely think, intent on nursing little wounds and a nasty scratch. Leander had reserved a seat for him, and Mauricio was touched by the gesture.

"You're red after the whole day under the sun without protection," Leander commented as soon as Mauricio sat down beside him.

"Is that why my skin's so itchy?" Mauricio wanted to scratch himself, but Leander stopped his hands with a laugh.

"I told you so! Maybe there's something here for irritated skin." He rummaged inside the multitude of pockets on his jacket. "You never know when even the silliest things will come in handy," he said, pulling out a small container. While showing Mauricio the tiny jar, he said, "It's an ointment; put it on your face later. Otherwise, you won't be sleeping tonight."

"Thanks, again." Mauricio took the jar and absentmindedly played with the lid.

It seemed to Mauricio that the trip back took even less time than it had in the morning. He enjoyed the short walk on the brick trail and breathed in the aromatic scent created by twisting several blades of grass between his fingers. He reached the cafeteria and got in line with Leander and the rest of the passengers of the van. They were the last ones to arrive, but Mauricio was relieved to see that there was some food left. Leander waved at Arias, who was sitting at a table with some other men. Mauricio waved too.

"There's some commotion tonight," Leander said, once seated at an empty table with his tray full of food.

Mauricio gave a distracted look around, but he didn't know what passed for normal around here. He was more interested in eating what he had put on his plate while it was still warm. At the Temple, though he had regular meals, his food was already cold when it reached his cell. He had never eaten with other people until his breakfast here, and he had all the intentions of enjoying his dinner now. He didn't care to hear about commotions or problems in general.

"Yes, there's definitely something going on." Leander wasn't eating. He had his fork dangling from his right hand and was looking, no, staring, at Arias.

Mauricio finished his food and regretted immediately not having taken more. The kitchen had closed soon after they had arrived, and now he was craving another helping of potatoes. He had never thought that potatoes, while still hot from the oven, could be so soft and tasty. Mauricio thought of only one thing he wanted more than a good meal, but it was impossible and he pushed the feeling away. Still, the thought of Rosie kept coming back since he had been forced to leave the Temple. Even while digging the trench, he thought of her and of her voice.

"I'm going to ask. You stay here; it won't take long," Leander said the last word already halfway between their table and Arias'.

Mauricio, having nothing to do now that he had licked his plate clean, finally took a better look at the rest of the cafeteria. There was some kind of excitement running through the room like a subtle buzz. Leander was talking to Arias animatedly. Mauricio kept his eyes on Leander until he came back with an expression he couldn't decipher.

"So?"

"The Presidential family is coming here. Tomorrow, they'll walk through the fields for the annual inspection." Leander sat down heavily and started toying with his food.

Mauricio, on the other hand, felt his stomach tightening and his heart racing. *But, she's still there at the Temple, isn't she?* he thought. "The whole family?" he couldn't help but ask.

"I don't know. Why would you care, anyway?"

"I don't."

"The presence of the President is bad news for the slaves. The women go crazy trying to demonstrate that this farm works better than the others, and we are forced to work shift after shift to clean the place. Last year was a nightmare. The President had the brilliant idea of saying that she liked a particular type of lavender Tarin didn't produce. We worked for three months to remove thousands of plants and replace them with the one the President liked. The day of the annual inspection, the chief guard showed her the fields with the new bushes, and do you know what the bitch said?" Leander asked rhetorically.

He just insulted the President. Out loud! Mauricio jumped on his seat and nervously looked around waiting for the guards to beat Leander unconscious, but nothing happened. Then he realized there weren't any women guarding the cafeteria. *How could I miss that?*

"How could you miss what? And why are you acting so weird?" Leander asked, following suit and turning right and left to see what had worried Mauricio.

"Did I say that out loud?" Mauricio looked at the other man who nodded up at him. "There are no guards here. How come there are no guards?"

"This is the men's cafeteria," Leander said with a matter-of-fact shrug; then when he saw Mauricio' s puzzled expression, he went on explaining, "They can barely stand our presence, let alone our smell, and this place is too crowded with men. They stay outside for the most part. After all, where we can go?"

"Ah, of course—"

"Anyway, what was I saying before you interrupted me?"

"Something about the President and the lavender fields?"

"Oh, yes… So, the President said her healer had recently suggested that she avoid lavender for a while, and do you know why?"

Mauricio didn't think Leander was asking him a real question and waited for the rest of the vent to come to its conclusion.

"Because the color purple didn't match her aura," Leander finished with a punch on the table.

Mauricio was taken aback by the man's strong, passionate reaction. *What should I say back?* His life at the Temple had been so far removed from human contact that he was unsure of what was expected of him. "That… sucks," he finally half-whispered.

"That's right. It sucked—"

Mauricio almost sighed in relief. *I got that right.* Although, his mind wasn't completely sold on the idea that the presidential visit was necessarily a bad thing. *Maybe Rosie is coming as well.*

"—and big time it did. Who knows what other whim of hers is going to destroy our peace?" Leander's question was answered immediately. A small army of guards ominously hovered just outside the cafeteria. The room went silent and the tallest of the guards stepped out.

"Arias," she called. The man stood up and let himself be known to her.

"You're taking care of two different projects: cleaning and beautification. For cleaning, you know the drill. For beautification, you'll work with the garden architect to create a design the President likes. Outside, there are two thousand roses to plant, and it must be done before dawn. Collect a group of forty slaves and meet me back at the entry." The guard turned around and the other women left with her.

As soon as the guards were gone from the room, the men started talking. Arias let them comment on the new orders for few minutes, probably while he was taking his time to decide who was going to work with him on the nocturnal project, and then raised one hand. Mauricio was surprised to see that Arias didn't have to raise his voice at all. Every mouth in the room stopped talking at the same time.

"As soon as I call your name, step forward." Arias followed with a list of names that didn't mean anything to Mauricio, until he called Leander and then Mauricio.

"Go take your bathroom break and come back here. We leave in ten minutes," Arias said and walked toward the restrooms without waiting to see if anyone was following.

Mauricio did like everybody else and was back in the cafeteria a few minutes later. He wasn't surprised that Arias had chosen him among the hundreds of slaves in that room. He was the newest addition to the group, and he was also young, like everybody else among the conscripted. Arias was the only one clearly not in his twenties. Leander wasn't happy about the whole situation and couldn't keep his annoyance to himself.

Mauricio, on the other hand, wasn't really mad. *Rosie could be here tomorrow*, he kept thinking. *And, I'm going to see what a rose looks like and how it smells.* His mind went back and forth between the desire to be in Rosie's presence again and his curiosity about the flowers.

"You'll see; this is the lavender disaster all over again. We'll skip a good night's sleep and we'll freeze to death for nothing," Leander said, his voice growing dangerously loud.

I ate too much and my skin feels too warm; some fresh air isn't going to hurt. "There's nothing you can do anyway." He gave Leander a shrug and waited quietly while the entry guards recalibrated their collars to let them out of the building.

After a short walk, more roses than he could have imagined were waiting to be planted. One of the guards who had escorted them outside opened the back door of a big van, and the smell reached Mauricio's nose with a punch. *Wow, it's intense. Rosie was right.*

"Be careful when you touch the stems. I don't want any of you slacking off tomorrow on account of a few cuts," the garden architect said. She turned out to be a woman with a mousy face and squeaky voice who ordered them around the whole night.

Soon enough, Mauricio's thoughts took a different direction. His fingers distractedly brushed a thorny rose stem. *Ouch, that stings! This isn't fun anymore and it's cold and my skin is itching even where the sun doesn't shine.*

In the middle of the night, Arias went around with pen and paper. "Whoever needs a restroom break better put his name on the list. It's the last break."

Mauricio raised his hand and noticed it was shaking.

"You go ahead," Arias said after taking a good look at him.

"Thanks." He got up on wobbling legs. Some of the men complained they needed to go urgently, too. He hurried through the process and was back in no time. He went down on his knees and cried, "OW! That hurts like a—" He stopped before it was too late; the garden architect raised her head from the blueprints.

"Take off your jacket, fold it in two, and place it under your knees," Leander whispered and pointed at his makeshift cushion.

Mauricio followed Leander's suggestion; it helped with the pain, but brought him near the point of freezing, although his skin was now on fire. Leander's ointment was the only reason he wasn't howling at the moon.

"What are you doing?" The garden architect loomed over him, whip at the ready. "I didn't call a break, or did I?" She kicked the ointment jar out of his hand and said, "Consider yourself lucky I can't waste my time punishing you."

Mauricio lowered his head, picked up the garden shovel and resumed working amid the most unnatural silence. He felt the other men's eyes on him; it wasn't a bad feeling and he drew some strength from it.

The garden architect let them drink every hour, not out of any consideration for them, but simply because she didn't want anyone to faint and leave for the infirmary.

"The President is going to love it when she sees the double-crown design from the airplane." Mauricio heard the garden architect murmur absentmindedly to herself, and when she left the blueprint on the ground by his side, he couldn't resist looking.

"What are you doing?" Arias hissed, his eyes glancing at the guard coming back.

"Nothing." Mauricio immediately resumed his position. The clear image of Rosie playing with her ring came back to his mind. *I wish you could see the roses I'm planting for you. You'd like them.*

"Why are you smiling?" Arias asked.

"I recognized the design," Mauricio answered before thinking better of it and regretted it.

"Everybody does; it's the Layan crest," Leander stated, and Mauricio was thankful that he didn't have to explain his words.

Meanwhile, the garden architect had realized the blueprints were lying on the ground and getting dirty. "Don't you dare put your hands on my project; keep your heads low and hurry. It's almost dawn already," she said to the men at large, but gave Mauricio a menacing look.

Leander scowled for everybody to see. Several men couldn't help sneering. Arias shot them a warning glance and Leander lowered his head when the garden architect turned to see what was happening. The first light of the day was shining in the sky when the last plant was carefully put to rest in its designated spot on the ground.

"Try to sleep now; your turn starts again in three hours," Arias announced when the garden architect dismissed them.

"I can't function on three hours of sleep," one of the men complained as soon as the woman was out of earshot. Several other voices joined the chorus of laments.

"Be glad that, in consideration of your hard work, I'm going to enroll someone else for cleaning duties," Arias said, effectively defusing the tension. Soon after, the guards escorted the slaves back inside and changed the calibration of their collars.

Mauricio found his drafty little room comfortable compared to outside. He closed his eyes and had the horrible feeling of being forcefully awakened seconds later.

"Time to go to work, sleepyhead," Guen chimed happily. She repeated the suggestion several times before Mauricio realized that she was talking to him, and that it wasn't, unfortunately, a nightmare.

He didn't say anything to her, just pulled on the work pants and found his way into a clean shirt.

"They pulled one on you last night," Guen commented while walking him to the back door. "The President remembers us only once a year. At least we are done with it now," she added with a tone that implied that the Presidential visits were a nuisance for her, too.

Mauricio wasn't going to say anything; he was barely awake and too tired from fighting his closing eyelids to muster anything smart and inoffensive to say about the President, but he was intrigued, nonetheless, by Guen's remark. He followed the woman, wondering how he was going to get through the day without collapsing when he sensed the guard stiffening suddenly.

CHAPTER 8

"Mistress, what an honor. What brings you to this wing of the building, and alone?" Guen's voice was barely under control. Mauricio turned around to see what was enraging Guen so much.

He heard the word 'mistress,' but he couldn't believe she was there, although he had fantasized about it the whole night; it was hard to accept that his dream had come true. He couldn't lower his eyes to the ground, as expected from a slave in the presence of a woman of Rosie's rank and status.

"I couldn't sleep and I wanted to go visit the gardens before the rest of the family woke up. I was told you added new flowers and that they are quite a sight," Rosie said while looking at him.

A mix of fear and happiness got hold of Mauricio's mind, and his senses grew sharper. He saw the light in Rosie's eyes become brighter and a touch of pink tinged her cheeks. He also felt Guen staring at the two of them.

"I am afraid it's not going to be possible, Mistress. It isn't wise to go outside by yourself, and the gardens are closed so early in the morning." Guen took a step forward and gave Mauricio a sharp look when he didn't move.

"But, I don't want to go back to my room. What am I going to do in the meantime?" Rosie positioned herself before the other woman.

"The chief guard is going to have a fit if she discovers the President's daughter is wandering through the farm without an escort," Guen murmured to herself, but loud enough to be heard.

"Nothing is going to happen to me in Tarin. Isn't it the safest farm in Ginecea? Or what they say about this place is not true?" Rosie smiled at Guen.

"Please, Mistress, go back to your room and wait until your personal escort comes to pick you up. It's the protocol." Guen sounded tired and resigned.

"I have a better idea. Since I'm already awake, and you are walking this slave outside, why don't I come with you? That way, I am properly escorted and nothing can happen to me. I see that you are very concerned about my safety, and I am sure you will protect me with your own life, if necessary." Rosie, who had started nicely and demurely enough, was back to her spoiled brat mode.

Mauricio's lips turned up slightly. Guen couldn't possibly deny the Mistress' request without being rude to the President's daughter. He felt as awake as Rosie proclaimed to be.

"Please, follow me," Guen capitulated, and after a last warning glance at Mauricio, she led the peculiar party outside.

Arias was on the other side of the back door, waiting for Mauricio. If he was surprised to see the President's daughter, he didn't show it. He lowered his head in a low bow when Guen indicated the honored guest with a nod and kept his mouth shut, as it was advisable for a man to do. Mauricio realized, belatedly, that he hadn't bowed, or showed any sign of respect, with the exception of not talking in front of Rosie. He knew Guen had noticed and he was also sure the guard must have noticed the lack of offense on the President's daughter's part.

"I think that it would be an educational experience for me, if I could follow the slaves throughout their schedule," Rosie said in her bratty voice, being very careful to sweeten her tone.

"Mistress, it is highly irregular. I know the President isn't—" Guen started to say.

"I can be my mother's eyes in all the matters she doesn't have time to supervise," Rosie said in a matter-of-fact voice, showing she meant business.

Mauricio wasn't sure how long Rosie could pull off her stunt, as soon as it was clear that she wasn't in her room anymore, a small army of worried security guards would storm over the entire facility to find her. *It's nice to have you here, even if for just a moment.* He felt physically better just having her close. He hadn't thought that was going to happen again, and he wasn't going to waste a free and unexpected respite from reality. He was dying of curiosity, though. How did she happen to be in Tarin with the rest of her family, given the web of lies she had woven to be in the Temple? It was difficult to have her here and not be able to talk to her.

"Very well, Mistress. Do you have any idea where you want to start your tour?" Guen's voice was controlled, but the undertone was loud and disrespectful. Rosie didn't seem to mind.

"I am not sure—" Rosie feigned some deep thinking and then genially smiled at Guen. "Where are these slaves going?" She pointed her small finger at Arias, as if she had just realized that the two men were there.

"Where are you headed today?" Guen asked Arias, and then added, "Slave?"

"Today, I am supervising the cleaning crew," Arias answered.

"Cleaning doesn't sound… interesting," Rosie said.

"There's a harvesting crew leaving in ten minutes for the mimosa fields. And, he—" Arias slowly turned toward Mauricio. "—is working at the trench up to the river border." He lowered his head while maintaining his voice deliberately without inflection.

"Mimosa flowers have the most pleasant scent. I'll ask the slaves to braid a garland for you," Guen tried to intercede.

"I am allergic to mimosa flowers. The powdery pollen makes me sneeze for hours," Rosie said in a worried tone.

"Do you want to see the river, then, Mistress?" Guen was at the end of her patience.

"I'd love to see the river." Rosie was satisfied and her lips turned slightly upward. She caught herself immediately and her face relaxed in a neutral expression.

Meanwhile, several men had come outside to start their day of work and were observing the scene from a safe distance. Leander was one of them. He kept looking at Mauricio, but he couldn't say anything directly to him while the high breed was there.

"Mistress, did you have anything to eat today?" Guen asked. "Maybe you'd like to go back to have some breakfast? We can go to see the river later."

"I'm not hungry, but thanks for asking." Rosie's face was a stony mask.

"We'll take a van by ourselves, then. You go ahead with your schedule," Guen said to Arias, who immediately dismissed himself and Mauricio. She called someone on her cell phone, and almost immediately, a van appeared at the end of the trail.

Mauricio couldn't stay without causing a problem for everybody. He followed Arias who was headed toward Leander but gave a sideways glance at Rosie before lowering his head; he saw her disappointment. He felt pleased that they could share that sentiment. At least they had that.

"So, what was that about?" Leander asked.

"The President's daughter has hijacked the guard for a private tour." Mauricio summarized the last half hour successfully without letting personal emotions slip.

"Pure breeds," Leander said. "The higher they are, the snottier they are."

"You can say that again," Arias said back.

Leander scoffed at the guard escorting the President's daughter, jumping to grant all of her wishes. Arias added a scornful remark aimed at the pure breeds and their utter evilness. Mauricio looked at the same women with a different feeling altogether and forgot to scoff in sympathy.

"Let's go eat something." Leander took Mauricio by his elbow and sauntered toward the cafeteria, where he took his time choosing what he wanted to eat.

Mauricio maintained a peaceful façade outside, but inside, he was screaming to Leander to hurry up and finish the damn toast and gulp whatever was left of the coffee. He ate everything he had put on his tray in less than five minutes and drank a steaming-hot beverage that was as bitter as coffee and left burns inside his esophagus. Leander was looking left and right and kept waving at people. He probably wanted to talk about the sleepless night with anybody who wanted to listen, but Mauricio had other plans for both of them.

"Let's go out working. I am feeling sleepy here. It's too warm," Mauricio said the first thing that came to his mind.

"Are you okay?" Leander was now looking at Mauricio.

"I'm fine. I ate too much and I need some fresh air." Words he had thought the previous night.

"And working is going to make you feel better?"

"Yes."

"Okay. Let me finish my coffee and we're out of here." Leander took a long sip from his cup and then, as promised, stood up to put away the tray with the empty plate.

"Thanks."

"Sure, no problem. If it makes you happy…" Leander said.

Mauricio noticed his inflection on the last part of the sentence, but his mind was elsewhere, too preoccupied to be bothered with subtle changes of tone. He walked down the trail, thinking only about the fact that Rosie had walked on this trail, too, just a few minutes earlier. He had just missed her. Only two days at Tarin, but he had thought of her constantly, imagined telling her about his new life. *Do you know my new cell has a tall ceiling and four circular windows? And, it's so cold… My guard's name is Guen; she told me that! Here, at Tarin, men have a cafeteria and they can eat as much as they want. Can you believe that? Oh… the fields… you must see the colors!* And now, she was here.

"I practically didn't sleep at all last night," Leander said to the fourth or fifth man who happened to cross his space.

Enough, already, everybody in this room knows about it.

"And, how much do you want to bet that the bitch hasn't even noticed." Leander had managed to stop a small crowd.

Really? Mauricio tried to move forward toward the door, but the discussion was still going. *I didn't sleep myself, but I'm not complaining. Am I?*

"No need to bet. I'm sure she didn't see anything," a man said.

Nobody asked for your opinion.

"What can you see from up there, anyway?" Another man pointed at the ceiling, meaning the sky.

"Imagine trying to see something on the ground from a plane!" Someone else felt the need to add to the conversation.

How could you know? Have you ever been on a plane?

"Exactly my point! The bitch could've blinked the same moment the plane was flying over Tarin's entry," Leander exclaimed.

Okay, you could be right on this one, but I don't care. Just keep moving. Like this, one step after the other. Meanwhile, Mauricio had dragged Leander outside, one comment at a time, without the man noticing the progress they were making. The journey from the cafeteria to the end of the trail where the van would pick them up was interrupted several times by men eager to keep talking to Leander. *Let's breathe before I punch him.* Mauricio tried to occupy his mind on something—anything that would calm his rising temper. He recognized every rock on the ground and every bush sculpted by the gardeners' hands. He counted blades of grass and every other man wearing dark pants, but his anxiety of getting out of there grew stronger. *Could I run to the trench? How long is going to take? Can I do it?*

"The van's just left. Good, we've at least ten minutes to relax," Leander said, a big smile on his face.

That's it. I'm going to punch you. But he didn't. *Stay calm, Mauricio. If you want to see her, you must stay calm.*

"What did you just say?" Leander asked.

"Nothing. I didn't say a thing. Look the van is coming back," Mauricio answered, his eyes focusing on the far away line that was the trench. *Just a moment. Be patient.* He hadn't realized how strong his feelings were until he saw her again. It was like they'd been simmering inside his heart, hidden from his consciousness. But now they were outside, and he couldn't get to the trench fast enough.

It took forever for the van to reach the river. Mauricio catapulted himself ahead of everybody else in the vehicle, a mélange of colorful insults accompanied his progress toward the exit, but he was the first one to get out.

Where are you? Mauricio scanned the place, his heart exploding in his chest. *Thank the Heavens,* he almost cried out loud when spotted Rosie's rich, chestnut hair. Guen was towering over her with outstretched arms explaining something, and Rosie was politely nodding. Mauricio was pleased to see in her brown eyes the same impatience he was feeling.

"And that, over there, is Bryn, the farm where the cotton for your clothes is produced," Mauricio overheard Guen saying in a bored tone. The guard wasn't making any attempt to hide what she thought of having to be there, instead of doing what her schedule called for.

"Mauricio! Come here, we need an extra hand hauling this rock," Grey called him from inside the trench.

Rosie's head turned around when she heard Mauricio's name. Mauricio saw Rosie's eyes illuminate when she saw him, and he automatically took two steps toward her. Grey's voice brought him back to reality, three times before Mauricio reacted to the call and fully faced the other way. The man waved at Mauricio to get to work. Mauricio couldn't do otherwise. Swearing under his breath, he went to help Grey.

"What are you, a sleepwalker?" Grey wasn't in a great mood.

"Yes, I am, since I had to work the whole night," he bit back, repeating Leander's words.

"I'm sorry for you. I really am. You'll get to rest later. Now get to work," Grey said, but at the last moment, he gave Mauricio a sympathetic shrug of his shoulders.

Mauricio knew that Grey couldn't cut him any slack before the other men and began digging without saying another word. He soon realized he didn't mind occupying his restless body on a physical activity when his thoughts were focused elsewhere. He felt Rosie's eyes on his back the whole time he worked, dislodging a heavy rock from its bed. He scratched his hands repeatedly, and blood came out of a superficial wound. Mauricio distinctly heard Rosie gasp when it happened. He felt immensely pleased by it and smiled. One of his coworkers looked at him.

"Are you okay?" the man asked him.

"Fine, never better," Mauricio answered.

"Maybe you should drink some water. You look dehydrated. I am going to fetch some for you."

"No! Thanks, I know where it is. I'll go. Walking will help clear my mind." Mauricio hurriedly put a hand on the other man's arm to stop him from going to the tanks that happened to be where Rosie was standing. The man gave Mauricio a worried look, but when he saw the determination in his face, he murmured something to Grey, who nodded, and Mauricio was let go.

Mauricio reached the closest tank to Rosie and went down on one knee to fill a plastic cup. Guen was giving a rather boring guided tour, but Rosie seemed to hang on the guard's words, asking questions and keeping the conversation going. Mauricio could almost feel the warmth emanating from Rosie's back while he took his time filling a small cup. They stayed frozen, back-to-back, unable to turn around and look at each other. Mauricio drank several cups of water while he noticed out of the corner of his eye that Grey was getting nervous, and that he and the man who had offered to fetch some water were looking at him impatiently. When he had almost given up and walked back to his crew, Guen's cell phone rang.

"Could you excuse me just for a moment, Mistress?" Guen asked Rosie.

"Sure, go ahead," Rosie answered maybe a tad too enthusiastically.

Mauricio couldn't see Guen's face since he was still facing the tank and the crew, but he imagined the speculative look on the woman's face at Rosie's thoughtless endorsement of leaving her alone in a field full of men. Guen murmured something and then Mauricio heard her steps growing softer.

"Is she looking at you?" Mauricio whispered while pretending to drink from the cup.

"Yes." Rosie stepped back a single long step that brought her closer to Mauricio's shoulders. Almost touching him. Almost. But enough to make Mauricio aware of every atom of air standing between them.

"Did you see the roses?" he asked.

"What roses?" Rosie replied and then, before he could explain, she said, "I missed you."

Mauricio stood frozen, incapable of speaking. Nobody had ever told him something so intimate.

"I know why you are here," she added, confusing him with her worried tone. "Don't say anything; just listen to me. My mothers know everything... about us. I was betrayed by the nurse who saw me outside your cell. She heard me talking to you and decided that she couldn't cover for my perversion. She didn't care to drag the Priestess along with me." Rosie was talking so fast that Mauricio had barely time to take in what she was saying.

"Did they do anything to you—?"

"No, of course not. Don't worry about me. Nobody is going to do anything to me. I am who I am, after all. I'll be fine. It's you I am worried about. The Priestess sent you to Tarin in an attempt to save herself. My mothers discovered what I was up to and flew to the Temple. They were furious with the Priestess for not having informed them about my... plan. And there was that recording..."

Mauricio was barely following her, and Rosie's voice was a whisper already, when she gasped, "The guard is coming back—" She moved away from him. "The nurse sent my mothers the recording where you entered my room, and they asked the Priestess for an explanation of why you were still alive. She answered that she had already disposed of you. But, I heard a conversation the Priestess had with my doctor, and I knew where she had sent you. I convinced my mothers it was a good idea to anticipate their annual visit here, but I feared I was too late..."

Mauricio could hear Guen's steps getting closer. Grey was walking toward him.

"It seems that you are too valuable as a semental to be killed right away, so the manager here has decided that some fresh air would improve your... skills... and then, when they have enough semen from you—" Rosie crammed the last words in a breathless sentence, but couldn't finish.

"Sorry for the interruption, Mistress. I had to take the call. It was your mothers' assistant. Needless to say, we have to go back immediately." Guen's voice was triumphant.

Mauricio felt cold when Rosie walked away, but he slowly took one step after another and met Grey halfway to the trench.

"I understand you're tired from a sleepless night, but I have a schedule and you're slowing everybody down. Just as a reminder, nobody gets to eat or sleep until we're done with the job. And the job today can't be done if we don't remove this rock from our path. Is it clear now why you have to get your act together and start doing something?" Grey was pinching the arch of his nose in a pose that betrayed a painful headache.

"Understood," Mauricio answered, lowering his head. He was sympathetic to Grey's plea. *Don't worry; I'm not going to be the one who makes everybody else suffer. I don't want to be a pariah, again.* The fact that Tarin seemed more humane than the Temple didn't mean that men weren't treated accordingly. *This is a slave farm, after all.* Absentmindedly, he touched the rigid collar around his neck. *I know who I am; this is a constant reminder of my condition. Even when I sleep, I'm not allowed to forget about this metal chafing my skin.* What was different now was that his mind was otherwise busy thinking about Rosie. *I shouldn't be thinking of her, at all. But, she has just told me that my life is in danger. How can I stop thinking about that?* He had to talk to her. He had to find her and eventually tell her that he had reasons to believe she was carrying his child.

Mauricio worked all day, doing what he was asked to do, nodding and saying whatever was expected of him depending on the tone of the conversation, but he wasn't present with the other men. *How am I going to find her, if I can't go anywhere by myself? And, even if I come up with a plan and find her, how am I going to say the things I need to say to her? And which one first? The only thing I know for sure is that I'll be choked to death as soon as I step outside the threshold of my cell. Time is running out; she's going to leave soon and I can't think of anything that will help…* These and other thoughts kept visiting him and left him exhausted.

Leander, who had watched him the whole day from inside the trench, went to talk to Mauricio when the shift finally ended. They were in line waiting for the van to come back and pick them up. "What's up with you?" he asked when it was evident that Mauricio wasn't in a talkative mood.

"May I ask you a question?" Mauricio said instead, facing the other man.

"It depends," Leander answered.

"You were a semental like me, right?"

"Yes—"

"Do the women ask you to produce?"

"Not anymore. Why?" Leander answered slowly.

"Because it seems that I am being fattened up, so to speak." Mauricio didn't like to dance around the words, but talking about his death sentence wasn't easy. Especially since he had a suspicion that the other man knew something about it. He had heard the same tone from both Arias and Leander, and somehow, things were beginning to make sense, in a macabre sort of way.

"I don't understand what you're saying," Leander tried.

"Thanks for telling me." Mauricio almost smiled.

"I didn't say anything."

"You did," Mauricio lowered his voice seeing that other ears were listening.

"I—"

"It's okay. You just nod." Mauricio stepped ahead with the rest of the line. It was their turn to get on the van. He walked to the first two free seats by the window and let Leander sit next to him.

"I know that I was sent to Tarin to die. The manager is waiting for me to be in better shape to exact one last production before being put to rest." Mauricio enunciated every word to be sure that Leander heard everything. Leander nodded, and he resumed his soliloquy, "The men have been asked to leave me alone. Arias appointed you as my personal bodyguard."

Leander nodded immediately this time. The van stopped, and again the drive hadn't lasted as long as Mauricio had hoped. It was either too long, or too short, but never right. He stayed in his seat a moment longer. "Am I missing something?" he asked Leander.

"I'm sorry, I can't—"

The men sitting behind them rudely asked them to stand up and get off the van.

"There's nothing I can do but keep you safe and make your life less miserable," Leander finished while walking out.

"Thank you, I guess." Mauricio followed the other man in silence. The cafeteria was full by the time they arrived. Arias was waiting for them by the door.

"You must come with me," the older man said with a somber expression. Mauricio had known him for less than two days and exchanged words with him only two or three times, but he could see that the man had something on his mind by the way he was walking. They went out and strolled around the cafeteria until Arias stopped behind a small tree.

"I want you to have this." Arias thrust a small object in Mauricio's hand as soon as they were out of earshot.

Mauricio took it and looked at Arias suspiciously. "What is it?"

"Something you might need. Drink the whole bottle if… things get too painful." Arias lowered his eyes to the ground.

Mauricio weighed the object in his hands and felt the whooshing of liquid. He held it before his eyes and, in the dim light, saw that it was a miniature flask.

"Why are you giving this to me?" he asked. He wanted the other man to say it.

"Because I can't do anything else for you," Arias' voice was a whisper, even though there was nobody out there with them but the wind moving through the trees, making their conversation difficult to hear.

"We need to go back. There are cameras everywhere." Arias took Mauricio's elbow and didn't give him any chance to ask questions.

They went back inside where Leander was waiting for them. Mauricio ate and was then escorted by both Arias and Leander to the main door; Arias saluted him with a trembling hand.

"Sleep well tonight," the older man said. Leander didn't utter a word, but gave Mauricio a look that was worth all he wanted to say.

Guen was already unlocking the door for him to come in.

"Are there other slaves on this floor?" Mauricio asked the guard abruptly. He knew it wasn't wise being disrespectful to a woman, but he was going to die soon, anyway.

The woman interrupted her stride for the briefest moment and then, without taking out the whip, answered him with a question. "Why do you want to know?" She looked straight at Mauricio.

"I saw that I am the only one escorted to this door. Nobody else seems to come here." Although he knew she wasn't the usual mean, spiteful guard, he could barely believe she was talking to him.

"You are a special guest," Guen said with a sad smile.

Mauricio's expression mirrored hers. She had just answered him, like Leander and Arias had done without having any intention to do so. "How long do you think I will be enjoying this special accommodation?" His voice was light, despite the bitter aftertaste that was rising up his throat.

"Not for long."

"Thanks for being nice to me."

"It was nothing," the woman said, but she looked uncomfortable.

"You care. It's a rare thing among your race." Mauricio kept talking. It hadn't been his intention, but somehow, the look in the woman's eyes had made him change his mind. "You don't like the President's daughter. Why?" He knew that asking such a question was pushing it too far, but he thought that it was worth a try to ask it anyway.

"How dare you?" Guen managed to sound shocked by Mauricio's liberty.

"Maybe it's not that you don't like *her*. Maybe you don't like the President." Mauricio was throwing caution to the wind, and he was so angry at his situation that he didn't care anymore. He hated that he was already considered dead. Arias had just tried to placate his own conscience by giving him poison. Or maybe the man had given him a strong painkiller. He didn't know what was inside the little flask tucked under the waistband of his pants.

"You better think twice before opening your mouth." Guen's eyes darted around before focusing once more on Mauricio.

He knew he had gone too far, but he couldn't stop thinking about the aversion Guen demonstrated while in Rosie's presence. The guard hadn't reacted to the requests Rosie made. Guen had reacted to Rosie. There was animosity in Guen's dealing with the President's daughter.

"I'm not going to talk to anybody, anyway." Mauricio dismissed the topic with a wave of his hand. He was grasping at straws, as if a slave's word mattered. The problem wasn't that he was talking too much; there was no danger in that for Guen. But plenty of trouble could come to her in the form of cameras and speakers hidden throughout the hallway. "I'm sorry if I've caused you any trouble." He turned slightly toward the guard and murmured for her ears only.

"You didn't sleep enough last night," Guen said, and then she seemed to realize they had been standing outside the slave's cell for several minutes and opened it for him.

Mauricio entered his *palace* and looked at the bare walls. "So, this is it," he said, facing the door where Guen was working on changing the frequency on his collar.

"This is it. Have a nice dream." Guen punched the last digit of the code securing him inside his cell, and before closing the door, she looked back at him one last time.

Mauricio caught the brief hesitation on the woman's face. Was Guen going to say something? Or was it regret, already? Did he really want to know? No, not really. He already knew enough. He felt paralyzed by the sensation of being unable to change his fate. Mauricio had always been conscious of his state as a slave, but he had decided to make the best out of it. Now he felt like screaming and yelling about the injustice of it all. And he didn't want to sleep through his last night on Ginecea.

"Mauricio?" A light tapping on the door woke him up.

Mauricio was surprised that he had fallen asleep after all. His name was repeated several times before he answered back.

"Rosie? What are you doing out there?" He was even more surprised that Rosie had found him.

"I wanted to talk to you," Rosie whispered.

"I'm glad you came." Mauricio sat on the floor by the door. He planted his bare feet on the cold tiles and waited for her to say something else. He imagined that she was doing the same on the other side of the wall.

"I hate that we can't be free to talk," Rosie said after a long silence.

"But at least you are here now." Mauricio put a hand on the door, and then he laid his forehead on the metallic surface, ignoring the tingling collar.

"My mothers are barely talking to me. They're worried that my pregnancy is going to reflect badly on them. Their publicist has been working non-stop to find a way to recover from this PR disaster." Rosie's voice was closer to the door now.

"What do you think she will come up with?" Mauricio felt some warmth seeping through the door where he had laid his hand. It was just his fertile imagination, but he liked to think that she was laying her hand on the other side.

"A nice girl from a nice family. The perfect wife to raise this child without scandals." Rosie tried to sound light, but even through the metal surface, the words came out anything but light. She sounded worried and ashamed.

"Do you already know her?" Mauricio banged his forehead on the door, slowly and deliberately. He was angrier than he thought he could possibly be after being told that he would die soon. Mauricio's stomach contracted to the size of a walnut. The sole idea of Rosie getting married to some "nice girl" was unbearable.

"I do. My mothers and hers have been trying to marry us off for some time now. Lavinia comes from an influential family loyal to my mothers' party, and it would be beneficial for everybody involved if we tied the knot," Rosie spoke slowly, and she seemed to be crying.

"Do you want to marry this girl?" Mauricio couldn't think straight. He wished he had the power to tear down walls.

"No! I already told you. I wanted to raise this baby by myself. Only us. It's not that Lavinia isn't a good person. She is, actually. But I don't love her. I've always looked at her as a good friend, but nothing more than that. I don't want to spend a lifetime with her. It wouldn't be fair to any of us." Rosie was crying and her voice came through the wall hoarse and sad.

"Who is…?" Mauricio wanted to ask her if she had changed her mind about raising the child alone, since she was using the past tense, but was afraid to ask.

"If it were possible, I would like to be with you." Rosie let out the words all together, barely breathing.

"There are cameras everywhere," Mauricio said, soon after his heart had started beating again. He wanted to say anything else but this. He wanted to confess that if he wasn't going to die anyway, he would have given his life just to spend time with her like they were doing now. He wanted to say that the pain he was feeling at knowing that she was going to be betrothed was the worst torture he had suffered in his whole life. He wanted to implore her not to marry, not to someone she didn't love. Not ever.

"I don't care," she answered, and Mauricio could hear that she was hurt by his words.

"But I do. They'll kill me soon, but you'll have to face the ire of your mothers. Your life will be ruined if the wrong ears listen to what you just said. Someone could use it to blackmail your mothers, and your life would never be the same. You'll be accused of perversion. There is no worse destiny for a woman, and you know it." Mauricio tried to explain the reasoning behind his apparent coldness. He didn't care about a President who kept him under slavery—and ironically, in any other occasion he would have rejoiced at the idea that *he* somehow could be the cause for the downfall of the purest of the Ginecean pure breeds—but he couldn't bear the idea that Rosie would suffer because of him. In a flash, he realized that he was betraying his race by trying to protect a woman.

"I wouldn't worry about my reputation being tarnished. I am afraid that my mothers already think the worst of me. I deceived them; I blackmailed the Priestess; I am pregnant…"

"Yes, but openly talking to a man is blasphemy," Mauricio interrupted her. "Aren't you worried of what could happen to you if this conversation is being recorded?"

"Even if someone is listening, I doubt that my mothers and the Priestess would gain anything by exposing me or making any of this public."

"Still, I don't understand why you are risking angering them over a slave. You don't even know me. We have only exchanged a few words." Mauricio couldn't believe that she was serious.

"Because I won't live with regrets. This could be the last time you and I talk to each other, and I won't waste the opportunity to tell you the truth. Not to save a reputation that isn't even mine. And because you are the only friend I have. You never saw me as the President's daughter. You never cared who I was. You accepted *me*. Not the brat, not the pure breed, just me. You never had anything to gain by our acquaintance, quite the opposite, actually. I caused your disgrace, and I feel guilty because of it. I don't want you to die. I can't accept that I am not going to see you again." Rosie was sobbing.

"Don't say that. You'll have a beautiful life. You'll have your baby to remind you of me." Mauricio hadn't planned to say it like this. Rosie fell silent. He had immediate second thoughts about revealing what he had put together.

"I'll always remember you," Rosie said tentatively.

"And I'll think of you as long as I'm alive." *I can promise that.*

"It's not enough for me," she replied softly.

"I'll always be with you," he said, thinking of the little baby growing inside her.

She started crying loudly at his last words. Mauricio decided that she had the right to know.

"Rosie, I'll be alive in your baby girl. Every time you look at her, you'll know I'm there as well. I'll never leave you," Mauricio said, hoping that she was going to let him talk.

"I don't understand..." Rosie had stopped sobbing, at least.

Mauricio felt it was a sign to keep going. "I heard the Priestess and the nurses talk about you and me. You know why I wasn't killed after I was found in your room?" Mauricio's feet were getting cold on the tiled floor. He shifted his body slowly to reactivate the sleeping limbs.

"I didn't think about it. I guess that they spared your life because they saw in the recording that you didn't mean to harm me."

He smiled at her words. Rosie's world was a good place to live in. "I was spared because they needed me to provide fresh sperm, in case you needed it. This is the only thing I'm good for." Mauricio hoped he wasn't too crude, but he didn't know how to say it without being direct, and time wasn't on their side.

"What—"

"Listen to me: Do you remember when you almost lost the baby?"

"Yes, of course."

"I was your private donor. They couldn't afford to lose me at that moment. Your pregnancy was at risk, and there wasn't any time to find another semental with the right genetics. I happened to match the list of traits you wanted in your baby." Mauricio didn't know how long they had left to talk. At any moment, Guen or someone else would come to check the floor.

"But it can't be! A man's semen is used only to conceive fathered women. Pure breeds go to the Temple to conceive with the help of the Priestess. She invokes the blessing of the Goddess, and the incognito descends on the women. Everybody knows that!"

"Every *woman* knows that..." Mauricio knew his words sounded blasphemous, but he had to tell his story. And when he was done, she could decide. "From what I heard, the Priestess uses the sementals to father both men and women. All women. Even the pure breeds." He heard her gasp and felt a pang inside. He wanted her to believe him. He hadn't realized how important it was to him that Rosie trusted him. Then a terrible thought flashed through his mind. At first, he refused to think it through, but after a few seconds, it formed again in his mind and he couldn't ignore it. What if Rosie was going to hate her baby? Could she still love her daughter if she knew that she was fathered?

Tears formed in his eyes, and for what seemed an eternity, he couldn't speak. Mauricio felt a longing to hold this little girl who wasn't born yet. He wanted to protect her, smile at her, and sing to her the lullabies his father had sung to him.

"What you said isn't believable. It's like saying that Ginecea is flat," Rosie commented at last, breaking the silence.

Mauricio was relieved by her words. She didn't sound like someone who was going to bolt in disgust. He breathed slowly, until he could steady his voice, and then told her everything he had put together. He started from the beginning, explaining the series of coincidences that had put him in a position to know what no man knew and probably very few women as well. Rosie listened in absolute silence. She must have had questions, but she waited for him to finish talking, and she was still there at the end of the tale.

"So, there is no incognito?" Her voice came out composed enough.

"I am your personal incognito." Mauricio rubbed his right temple with sweaty fingers. Talking was taking its toll on his mind and body. It was the second night in a row with little or no sleep at all, and he was going on pure will. "It's the only reason I've been spared death, until now…"

"Don't say it."

"It's the truth. You are fine, the baby is fine, and I'm not needed anymore."

"I don't want to listen to this. I don't want to listen to anything."

"I'm sorry, but you had to know. I wanted you to know."

"The things you're saying are blasphemous—"

"You'll have time to think about what I told you. You don't have to believe me now, but promise me you'll think about it." Mauricio waited for Rosie to answer back, and when she didn't say anything, he thought she had finally left. "Please," he said to the wall.

"I am trying," she whispered.

"It's the only thing I ask of you."

"So, you are saying that there are no differences between pure breeds, fathered women—" Rosie paused longer than Mauricio thought was a good sign and then resumed with a lower voice, "— and men. No… it can't be. It simply can't be…"

A muffled sound came from outside. Mauricio didn't know what to think about Rosie's silence, and then he heard the steps coming closer.

"Mistress? Going for a stroll?" Guen's voice was higher than necessary.

"I don't usually sleep well at night, and now the daily sickness and the nausea have also started. Walking relaxes my nerves and gives me time to think," Rosie answered calmly.

"I'm not sure how much relaxation you can achieve walking around this dreary place. This is not the most beautiful area of the compound. Tarin is renowned for its immaculate fields, but not for the elegance of the interiors," the guard commented with a sarcastic tone. "There's nothing interesting here," she added with a sudden change of tone.

Mauricio had the distinct feeling that Guen had seen Rosie talking to the wall of his cell, probably from a comfortable seat inside the surveillance room. She was playing with Rosie. Any moment now she would call her bluff and expose her.

"Mistress, I think I have a solution for your problem. I'm at the end of my turn. I'll accompany you to the terrace, where you can have a private view of the sun rising over the fields, if you like the idea. I assure you the sight is dramatic," Guen said, and just as she said it, other steps echoed in the silent hallway. A few greetings were exchanged and Guen officially passed the baton to the next guard.

Mauricio remained a few seconds on the floor, not really sure of what to make of Guen's actions. He was worried about her intentions. He fought the nervousness that was reducing his ability to think straight and went to lie down on the bed. He tossed and turned on the uncomfortable surface for a long time, and only when Tarin started to wake up did he close his eyes.

CHAPTER 9

A guard who wasn't Guen woke him up. She wasn't gentle in the execution and seemed to enjoy having to activate the collar to convince Mauricio that it was time to go to work. *She could have powered it up another two notches,* he thought, trying to find the bright side of the stinging burn on his neck. He was out of the cell in mere seconds, and the collar returned to a comfortable buzz. Mauricio automatically turned toward the door opening onto the fields. Arias was already there, peering through the window, waiting to escort him to the cafeteria.

"Other plans for you." The guard redirected Mauricio to another hallway.

He saw the distressed look on Arias' face and saluted him with a nod, mouthed, *thank you,* and even tried to smile at the other man. Arias' eyes stayed on him until he turned around a corner. Mauricio dragged his legs after the guard, his mind jumping to the conclusion that he was being led to the slaughter. They walked for several minutes through a series of well-lit chambers, and then the guard slowed down before a glass door.

"Now, you'll do what you do best." She pointed at a low table with a tray full of plastic cups, waited long enough to be sure he understood, then left, sliding the glass door shut behind him.

Mauricio took a depressed look at the room. *I was born and raised in a place like this, and I'm going to die in a place like this.* He sat down on the customary white chair and took one cup in his hand. *This is all I'm worth to them.* He gingerly tossed the cup from one hand to the other. *I'm not going to make it easier for you.* He couldn't have, even if he wanted to. *Now that I know the truth, I want to make a difference. This'll be my last act of rebellion before dying. I was born a slave, but you are going to slaughter a free man.* Mauricio put the cup back on the tray with the others.

He started playing with them, rearranging their order until he was satisfied with the result. *I'm sure after today, you'll remember my number.* Then he stood up and knocked on the glass door.

"Done?" The guard appeared from around the corner.

"Yes. I am definitely done with this," Mauricio answered. *You have no power over me anymore.*

The guard looked at him for the first time since she had come to his cell and then looked at the tray.

"What does that mean?" she asked, enraged.

"Exactly what it looks like." Mauricio smiled proudly. *This feels good.*

"You… you…" The guard was in shock; a slave had dared to defy a woman's direct order. She was staring at the tray with the cups neatly aligned to spell the word 'no' and no other sounds came from her mouth.

Mauricio knew that there was a camera somewhere in the room and fervently hoped that later, when the guards analyzed what had happened there, they would see how happy he was at that precise moment. *Look at me; look at my face. You've never seen me before; I'm a new breed of man.* He turned around slowly, facing every wall to be sure that his smile couldn't possibly be missed. He was down on his knees a few seconds later, but before passing out, he thought, *At least you gave me enough time to do a full rotation; it should be enough,* and then thanked the guard out loud.

* * *

He opened his eyes, knowing right away that he was in his cell. The first thing he saw was the high ceiling looming over him. He didn't bother to move. The collar was mercilessly scratching the blistered skin of his neck, and he had probably woken up because of the pain that was making him cry even while he slept. His muscles were having spams, and he knew from past experience that he had to let it pass. Through the pain, Mauricio's lips managed to twitch in a vague smile when recent memories of how he had ended up in his cell came back. *I've defied a woman's orders, and I'm still alive. I can't be dead and feel so much pain.*

A strange smell in the air interrupted Mauricio's thoughts. It was a sweet scent that invaded his nostrils and his throat. Mauricio saw white smoke coming out of the four little windows in the walls. His eyes, already watery, started stinging. He felt his throat constricting, and panic took over. Before dark patches covered his vision of the tall ceiling, the white fog filled his cell and the sweetness in the air became horrid. Mauricio coughed until his throat felt like a floor of broken glass. He brought his hands to the collar in an irrational attempt to loosen the grip on his skin. When he couldn't cough anymore and his mouth froze in a silent scream, he thought of the tiny baby girl he knew was his daughter and fainted.

* * *

From far away, Mauricio heard a commotion of metallic sounds, human steps, and voices calling him, but he didn't react. How could anybody ask more of him? Why wouldn't the voices leave him alone? And what was it with all the beams of light cutting through his eyes?

"He's not responding." He heard a familiar, feminine voice say. Frantic. Worried. *For me? Why? I'm beyond pain and misery. Leave me alone. I deserve to be pain free for once in my life.* "I can't move him. He is too heavy for me."

"Get his arms. I'll get his legs," another voice ordered. Equally familiar, but older.

Mauricio opened one eye, but it was dark. There were cones of cold light cutting through the obscurity, but his head was bent at an odd angle and he couldn't see anything.

"How long do you think it's going to take them to restore the electricity through the main building?" Rosie's voice sounded as if coming from underwater.

Mauricio was slowly regaining consciousness. He was still disoriented and queasy. A throbbing ache enveloped his body, making it difficult to think.

"Not more than ten minutes. Probably less. We have to hurry." He recognized Guen's muffled voice. A loud thud reverberated inside Mauricio's ears.

Rosie cursed, saying, "I dropped my light. I can't see where I'm going."

"Calm down. Follow my voice. I'll aim my light higher, so it illuminates the vaults." Guen sounded calm. Mauricio automatically relaxed at the sound of the older woman's voice giving instruction to Rosie.

"We're almost there. I can see the door. Lay him down. I have to cut his collar before we go out," Guen explained. After a moment she said, "Okay, slowly, careful not to bend his neck too much. Keep the light straight at his face. Yes, good, like this. Just a moment now—" Guen grunted and then he heard a small *snap*. "—perfect, just perfect. The seam just gave way. Now, to cut through the material... and... done." Something fell on the floor and the guard sighed in satisfaction.

Mauricio felt the skin on his neck getting colder, and then he realized that the collar wasn't there anymore.

"Okay, give the light back to me and take care of him while I signal to Arias that we are ready." Guen left Mauricio's side.

"Rosie?" he croaked.

"Mauricio!" Rosie was close to his face, but everything was dark again.

"Shhh!" Guen whispered from somewhere.

"Mauricio, I was scared that it was too late," Rosie whispered in his ear.

"How..." Mauricio was still too tired to formulate whole sentences, but Rosie understood his question anyway.

"I heard my mother giving the order to get rid of you. Someone besides Guen noticed my escapade two nights ago."

"Two nights..." Something loud was banging inside Mauricio's head, but he thought he had heard correctly. *How long have I been out?*

"They kept you asleep while withdrawing... what they wanted from you. My mother doesn't think that you are really worth the trouble, and today she decided that whatever they had was going to be enough."

"Guen?" Mauricio was struggling to stay awake when his mind and his body wanted to faint. *Why is a guard helping a slave?*

"Guen... it's a long story. I'll tell you everything later. For now, what matters is that you are alive, thanks to her, and that you can trust her." Rosie stood up at the sound of faraway steps. "Guen?"

Mauricio felt the floor vibrating with a stampede of steps and shuddered.

Rosie put a hand on his shoulder and squeezed softly. "I think I see Arias. Yes, there he is. I'm going to open the door. Be ready to haul him out. We don't have much time left before the guards arrive," Guen said. The whoosh sound of the door seemed louder than usual.

"Hurry!" Arias called from outside.

"Can he walk?" Guen asked, while coming back from the door.

"No, he keeps dozing on and off," Rosie answered.

I'm here.

Guen made a guttural sound when she tried to raise Mauricio's body from the floor. "We need help; he's too heavy for the two of us."

"I can't come in. The dorms outside of the main building have a different power supply. My collar hasn't shut down." Arias was frustrated.

Guen swore loudly. "I hadn't thought of this—" And she swore again.

"We're going to make it." Rosie breathed hard and then raised Mauricio by his shoulders. They took a few steps and were almost at the door when Mauricio's body was shaken by a sudden tremor. Guen lost her grip on his legs and let him down. Rosie was dragged to the floor beneath him.

"I hear voices. Hurry up, now!" Arias was getting anxious. The steps were getting closer.

"Be still, please." Rosie was now crying.

I can hear your heart racing, Mauricio thought, feeling comforted by her proximity.

"Now!" Arias was yelling.

"Are they coming for him?" Rosie asked.

"I'm afraid they've already discovered he hasn't died. When they gassed the chamber, they also activated a vital-alarm." Guen helped Rosie move Mauricio out of the way. "I had hoped we had more time."

Stop talking so loud; my head hurts. But his wish wasn't granted; nobody cared about being quiet anymore. Rosie's, Arias', and Guen's voices were drowning under the noise of the guards running toward them

Guen and Rosie made a final, desperate attempt at carrying Mauricio outside. Arias reached his arms inside, and the shock from the collar kicked in. He screamed, but still managed to help the two women haul Mauricio through the door. Once outside, the older man relieved Guen and Rosie of their cargo, took Mauricio in his arms and started running.

"I'll catch up with you later. I'll try to buy you some time by locking the door from here." Guen's voice became fainter as Arias put some distance between the main building and them.

Mauricio wanted to throw up; his head was being tossed every which way, and his neck was bleeding.

"Don't give up. We've almost reached safety." Rosie was running along with Arias.

Mauricio hooked his mind to Rosie's voice and used it as an anchor to remain conscious. He could feel the cold air of the night biting at his skin, which also helped. Finally, Arias stopped running and put him down on the ground.

"Are you too cold?" Rosie was immediately by his side.

No, I don't feel cold.

"Are you in pain?"

"Yes," he managed to answer.

"Is it too much? Can you bear it?" She was talking fast. "Arias, I don't think he can bear it. He's shivering."

"I don't know..." Mauricio couldn't finish the sentence. *My tongue is swollen and my lips are cracking every time I try to say something. Is this normal?* "I'm happy—" *I got to see you one last time.*

"He's not making any sense," Rosie cried.

I'm fine; don't worry, he wanted to say, but his eyes were closing despite his efforts to remain awake.

"He fainted," Rosie cried.

No, I haven't; I'm still here.

"It is a normal reaction to the gas they pumped inside his cell. He's going to be fine," Arias answered.

Am I?

"Are you sure?"

"Yes. Don't worry, Mistress," Arias said.

You don't sound so sure, do you? Mauricio laughed.

"Arias, is he crying? Is it the pain?"

"His body is trying to release the toxins."

"What are we waiting for?" Rosie took one of Mauricio's hands in hers.

Your skin is so soft and warm. I feel better already. His mind was slowly starting to clear, but he was still confused about what was happening around him.

"We are waiting for Leander to jump start the van and pick us up here," Arias answered Rosie, but he was preoccupied and it showed in the way he spoke.

"What if—" Rosie started while stroking Mauricio's hand.

"Don't think about that, Mistress. Leander is coming."

Mauricio could hear the older man pacing back and forth. Rosie was stroking his hand absentmindedly, but the prolonged silence between her and the slave was difficult to ignore. The surreal atmosphere was broken by the ominous sound of angry voices rapidly approaching.

"Arias, the guards are already here. Where is Leander?" Rosie stood up alarmed.

"Rosie..." Mauricio murmured when her hand left his. *Come back.*

"I won't let anything happen to you. I promise," Rosie crouched down immediately and whispered to him.

"I see Leander. I see him!" Arias shouted and then came to help Rosie with Mauricio.

"Where is Guen?" Rosie asked with sudden apprehension.

"We have to leave as soon as the van arrives." Arias put his arm under Mauricio's armpit and pulled him up. "Man, you've got to help us. Stand up," he coaxed.

"Mauricio, hang in there. It's just for a little while longer." Rosie went to the other side and tried to keep him standing.

"I can hear the engine," Rosie said to Mauricio.

Mauricio felt the van coming through the vibrations under his feet. He opened his eyes, but it was still too dark to see anything farther than his nose. Rosie faced the incoming vehicle and he turned with her.

"I'll be right back; I need both hands to light a match to help Leander find us." Arias cautiously removed his support.

Mauricio felt it immediately, but he tried not to fall on Rosie.

He saw the light showing through Arias' fingers, and for a moment, the night was less dark. The match consumed itself faster than Leander could have possibly seen it. Arias lit a second one and then proceeded to light another three before the sound from the van's engine got increasingly closer. Meanwhile, the shouting voices were getting louder. Mauricio's heart was pounding with adrenaline; not knowing where the guards were was torture.

Finally, the van arrived. Arias came back to support Mauricio, and the three of them ran toward the vehicle.

"What took you so long?" Arias yelled as soon as Leander opened the passenger's door.

"It's not like I steal cars every day, you know? And, I couldn't find the gasoline tanks you asked for." Leander's face was illuminated by a faint light, and his hands were shaking on the wheel. "Good thing the women needed someone to get rid of the sewer waste, or they would have never taught me how to drive."

"Thanks for coming to my rescue," Mauricio murmured.

"Anytime," Leander answered without smiling.

Arias let Rosie inside first and then helped Mauricio by her side. "Lower the seats down," he instructed Rosie, and then he climbed in beside Leander. "Go!" he commanded.

"But, what about Guen?" Rosie asked.

"Guen knew what she was doing," Arias answered, while giving the final okay to Leander to start the van. The window by his side cracked.

"What the—" both Arias and Leander said at the same time.

Mauricio gingerly touched the pieces of broken glass now resting on his lap; he watched as a trickle of blood dripped down from his fingers.

CHAPTER 10

"Are you hurt?" Rosie took Mauricio's hands in hers and cleaned off the blood.

I feel... strange.

"Is he hurt?" Arias turned around and swore at the sight.

It can't be that bad. I'd feel way worse.

"No, he isn't," Rosie answered after a cursory inspection of his body.

It tickles where you just touched me.

"Go, don't stop for anything," Arias said to Leander, who did as ordered and the van's tires screeched on the ground.

Why are you trembling? "Are you okay?" Mauricio, with great difficulty, asked Rosie.

"I'm fine," she answered, but her shaking body said otherwise.

He rested his head on her shoulder. *I'd hold your hand if I only could raise mine.* He looked down at his body, but nothing seemed wrong with it. "What—"

Another crack and the van swerved dangerously to the right, sending all the passengers across the seats.

"Take control of the van!" Arias shouted above the deafening noise coming through the broken window.

"I'm trying!" Leander answered, his voice shaking. Another loud *crack* and the van circled around on its axis. "What's... oh crap—" Leander didn't see the large stone in their path until it was under one of the tires that had not yet been shot out. He lost control and the van went flying.

Mauricio was freefalling inside the revolving vehicle. He hit the ceiling with his head, and then his limbs followed. Rosie's body tangled with his. Somebody started screaming. The van kept rolling for what seemed hours and then finally stopped.

I feel nauseous.

"Get out of the van. Now. Or I'll shoot you where you are." A woman was staring at them upside down. Another four were standing several steps behind the speaker, upside down as well.

That's strange...

"We're trapped," Arias said.

"Are you wounded?" the woman asked.

"My arm is broken," Arias answered.

"And you?" The woman poked Leander with the tip of a rifle. Leander stayed motionless. The woman poked him again. "I guess this one is gone. Good riddance to him," she said, and without spending more time on Leander, moved to the side and looked at Mauricio. "Are you dead, too?" She was still walking upside down. "This one is trapped against the ceiling." The woman called someone else to help her.

Mauricio felt their hands tugging and pulling at some parts of him, and then he fell down and the universe rearranged itself. Now the woman was standing right.

"Mistress Layan!" she yelled in surprise when she realized who the fourth passenger was. The women rushed to help extract Rosie from the vehicle.

"Is she alive, Captain?" one of the four women asked with a terrified voice.

"She's breathing and there's some blood on her hands and on her shirt, but I think she's fine," the woman with the rifle answered, relieved. "Call her mothers, immediately," she commanded, and someone scurried away. "Mistress?"

Mauricio saw the woman lay the rifle down, put Rosie on her lap, and slap her gently.

What are you doing? Put her down!

"Mistress? Can you hear me?"

Rosie stirred and opened her eyes. She screamed and scrambled out of the woman's embrace.

"Mistress, I'm Captain Reese. It's okay. You're not in danger anymore; we just rescued you, and we have called your mothers. They're coming."

Rosie looked at the woman, and it was clear in her eyes that she was horrified. The captain mistook Rosie's behavior and leaned in to comfort her. "Don't touch me," she screamed.

At hearing Rosie's distress, Mauricio commanded his body to react, and after a moment of struggling, he was able to escape from one of the broken windows. With great effort, he hauled his body out of the van and then dragged himself to Rosie, using only his arms. *I sure could use my legs right now.*

Both Rosie and the captain saw him, and for a moment, silence reigned. The captain went for the rifle, but Rosie slapped away the woman's hands, sending the arm to the ground, and ran toward Mauricio.

"Shoot him," the woman ordered the group of hesitant guards.

Rosie heard the command and impulsively covered Mauricio with her body.

No! Don't! He tried to move her, but he didn't have any strength left.

At the same time, the captain saw what was happening and let out a string of swear words. "Stop! Do not shoot. I repeat, do not shoot!" The woman stood up and faced the guards, who were aiming at the bodies on the ground. "Mistress, please stand up. We are here to defend you. Let us do our job," she spoke slowly.

Mauricio saw how, while the captain was talking to Rosie, she was silently commanding her guards to come closer and, with a hand gesture, was positioning them in a semicircle. "Rosie, you must get out of here," he whispered to her, but his voice was so low he didn't know if she could hear him. *You must save yourself and our baby.*

"You are in shock; please move away. This slave is a fugitive. You must listen to me for your own sake, or this man is going to harm you," Captain Reese said in the sweetest voice, as if she was talking to a small child.

Rosie didn't acknowledge the captain's words, instead she whispered to Mauricio, "I'm not going anywhere and I won't let her take you."

"She's going to kill—" *I want you and the baby to live.*

"Mistress Layan, please, listen to me. It's done… You're safe now, *with us*." The captain stressed the last two words. "A doctor will check you as soon as we get back to the building." She took a small step toward Rosie, while accepting a gun from a guard.

"Don't come any closer," Rosie called back without looking at her, and then her mouth was pressed to Mauricio's ear again. "I'll find a way out of this. I promise."

"How? Go away, now." Mauricio moved and his mouth was aligned with hers. His heart slammed against his chest and he felt dizzy.

The captain looked back and forth between Rosie and Mauricio, her eyes becoming wider as she took the whole scene in. "Mistress? What are you doing? Are you okay?"

"Leave us alone. Go back to the farm," Rosie said, her hands splayed on Mauricio in a protective gesture.

"I can't do that. I'm sorry. You need to let me do my job, so step away from the slave, like the good pure breed you are." Captain Reese started to walk toward Rosie, and the rest of the women moved along, corralling her and Mauricio inside the ring.

"Rosie… you should go…" *Whatever you intend to do, the captain isn't going to let me live anyway, but you don't need to suffer because of me.* Mauricio tugged at her arm. The effort of staying conscious was consuming all of his energy, and thinking and talking at the same time was already a chore.

"No, I shouldn't. I got it—don't worry; they are not going to shoot at me." Rosie put one hand on his arm to reassure him. "If you want him, you have to go through me," she said to the guards.

Mauricio felt her shivering. "Rosie…" he tried to say something, but he was losing his grip on reality.

"This is not happening," Captain Reese said, dangerously moving her gun from one hand to the other. "Why would you care if anything happened to a slave?"

"You wouldn't understand," Rosie answered the rhetoric question.

"No, obviously, I wouldn't." All of a sudden, Captain Reese retraced her steps and went to haul Arias out of the vehicle. "But, I can play your game," she yelled and angrily pulled at the man's arms while he screamed in pain. She said something back to Arias and then pulled some more. She was satisfied only when his body was completely out on the ground where Rosie could see what she planned to do.

"No!" Rosie yelled as soon as the captain pointed the gun at Arias' back.

Mauricio started trembling. *I don't want anybody else to suffer.*

"Now, let's see if we understand each other," the captain said, looking coldly at Rosie. A ringtone echoed in the night.

"Captain, Bruna, the President's publicist, wants to talk to you." One of the guards interrupted her and, ignoring her incinerating glare, offered the woman the cell phone.

The captain snatched it from the guard's hands and whispered angry words at the caller. Using the same irritated tone, she briefly explained that she had the fugitives and the President's daughter, who didn't want to cooperate. The captain stared at the night sky while the other person took her time to comment. The expression on her face betrayed a whole array of different feelings. Anger was replaced first by shock, then astonishment, and finally, incredulity.

"What you are suggesting can't possibly work," the captain said after a long pause. She looked around as if worried that someone was eavesdropping to her conversation. "And, pray tell me, how do you think I am going to explain it to the President?" the woman said between clenched teeth. "This is a nightmare," she added, while abruptly closing the cell phone. Arias, still under the gun's aim, moaned in pain. Without announcing her intentions, the captain hit him hard in the head with the butt of her gun. Arias lay still.

Mauricio shook with tremors and automatically reached for Rosie, seeking her warmth, but then belatedly realized he wasn't supposed to do that and put his arm back to his side. *Sorry, I didn't mean to put you in any more trouble...*

"Hang in there," she said and, without a second thought, took his hand in hers.

He shook his head, but left his hand where it was, closing his eyes to imagine a happier situation. *You make me feel I'm worth something.* "Thank you."

The captain's harsh voice brought him back. "Well, I tried my best not to let things reach this point." She looked at the gun and then changed aim. The weapon was now pointing at Rosie, who was wrapped around Mauricio.

Mauricio tried to straighten his head and saw from the look in her eyes that the captain was furiously thinking. *What did the publicist suggest you to do?* He didn't like the way the captain was acting; the woman was mumbling words while her gun was still targeting Rosie. In the distance, he heard the sound of another car coming, and he saw her investigate the new arrival.

The woman looked less composed than she had been before the phone call. She finally lowered her gun and began to pace back and forth, repeating the same sentence several times. "It could work. If I do it right, it could work." The captain wiped the sweat from her temples and looked at Rosie still protecting the slave. She shuddered in revulsion and resolution dawned on her face like a mask. She breathed slowly and then went back to Arias' side, raised his limp hand and pressed her gun into it. Then she directed Arias' armed hand until it aimed at Rosie. "If you are not well, you need help. I'll put you down," she said, her voice as cold as ice, then pressed her hand on Arias' fingers and steadied her stance.

All at once, people started screaming. The four guards were looking horrified at their captain. But one voice was louder than the others.

"No! She's pregnant. The President's daughter is expecting a child!" Mauricio shouted while Rosie was pressing down on his chest. The four guards gasped and two of them instinctively ran toward their captain to stop her.

"What?" the captain said, stunned that her own subordinates were revolting against her orders. Then a cruel smile lit her face and she raised one hand to put a halt to their betrayal. "Idiots! Don't you see that it's just perfect? Imagine the tragedy. I can read the news already. 'Tarin's facility attacked by slaves. Pregnant Rosie Layan dies. Ginecea is shocked by the senseless violence and forces the mourning President to pass the laws to limit slaves' rights.' It couldn't work better." She resumed the stance and added as an afterthought, "And clearly we are in need of better legislation to deal with these animals."

Mauricio squeezed Rosie's hand. "I'm so sorry."

"I'm not," she said, easily counteracting his feeble attempt to put her out of harm's way.

"Rosie… " He wanted to say many things, but words escaped him. He bent his head toward hers to inhale her scent. *My little rose without thorns.*

"Mauricio…"

"Bruna is right. Your mothers are better off without you. You are an abomination," the captain said.

"I'm ready," Mauricio whispered, facing the woman. *But she's not.* He channeled all his strength toward his hands to push Rosie away.

The captain's hand never completed the act of pressing Arias' fingers on the trigger. A rock landed heavily on her head before she could shoot. The woman emitted a choking sound and fell to the ground. Leander emerged from the darkness behind her, looking aghast. He was staring at the pool of blood seeping from the captain's motionless body. Heedless of his surroundings, he didn't notice the guards coming at him from the side.

"Leander, watch out!" Mauricio barely had time to say it before one of the guards struck the young man with the butt of her gun. Leander fell facedown in the blood.

"Stay down." The guard gave Leander a kick for good measure. She was hysterical. The rest of the women stood still, uncertain of what to do with the President's daughter. Not one of them dared aim her gun at Rosie.

"I need help here." The guard who had struck Leander repeated the message several times on her radio. Once she was certain that someone had received it and that the slave wasn't going to stand up any time soon, she turned toward her captain. She mumbled something under her breath that sounded like a prayer, and then she gingerly touched the captain's arm. One of the other women asked her if the captain was alive.

"I can't feel her pulse... no wait... yes, she's breathing." The guard exhaled loudly. Several other comments of relief followed from the side.

The harsh sound of tires quickly stopping on the gravel made all those present turn around immediately. The guard stood, ready to confront the newcomers. A car skidded to a halt before the upside down van.

"Identify yourself, recruit." A woman in her sixties with a deep voice and a large gun positioned to fire walked toward the group composed of four bodies on the ground, one woman standing and three other women looking like beaten dogs.

"I am Cadet Byne, Colonel," the guard whispered and let her gun fall as she raised her once-armed hand to salute the higher-ranking woman.

Leander's arm shot out in the direction of the gun, but the older woman was faster and snatched it without any effort, kicking him in the face as an afterthought. Then she commanded the cadet to recount what had happened. When she was satisfied with the tale, she dismissed the younger woman as utterly incompetent. Without breaking eye contact with the group, she stepped back, reached her car, and talked to someone inside. She waited until the women got out and retraced her steps, while aiming both guns at the slaves.

"Look who's here. My mothers' infamous and efficient publicist." Rosie, who had kept silent the whole time, spoke calmly, as if resigned. "Have you come to fix things as usual?" she asked.

"I think that you actually like it. Otherwise, why else would you be such a pain in my ass?" A woman wearing a business suit glared at Rosie and then turned around to speak to the colonel.

"Nobody here saw anything. Is that understood, Colonel? Invent some night drill and put it on paper. I'll sign it," the business suit said.

"Not so fast, Bruna. I won't let you get away with whatever you're planning." Rosie moved to face her, still shielding Mauricio.

"What is it now? Getting pregnant wasn't enough fun for you? You needed to transgress some more? You really want to end your mother's career, don't you?" Bruna flattened a wrinkle on her skirt. "You had to choose perversion as your new hobby. What about the usual: drugs, gambling, and cheating on your tests, like every other good society girl? No, that was too much to ask. But, I almost admire you. You went beyond any expectations I had. You have outdone yourself this time. Congratulations. Now, shut up and let me clean up your mess. As usual."

"Where are my mothers?" Rosie asked.

"I wasn't going to wake them up for *this*!" Bruna pointed a finger at the slaves and looked utterly disgusted. "You've already aged them twenty years with all the shenanigans you've put them through." She looked at Rosie with pure contempt. "We are going to deal with this situation quietly. And you are going to collaborate with me."

Mauricio, after a sudden moment of clarity, used all the energy he had left to slowly stand up and step outside of Rosie's shield.

"Don't!" She followed him and automatically started rearranging her position to protect him.

Mauricio squeezed her arm gently and stopped her where she was. "It's okay. You have done more for me than I could've possibly asked any other human being to do. I am grateful I lived long enough to get to know you," he whispered to her and then moved aside to expose himself completely.

The colonel took advantage of Rosie's momentary confusion. The older woman rested one of her guns on Mauricio's temple and cocked it. Rosie flinched at the sound.

"Don't shoot him," Rosie cried and fell to her knees. "I beg you, please don't shoot him."

Rosie, no...

"You are pathetic." Bruna marched toward Rosie and pulled her up. "Colonel, kill him and the other two slaves and then clean up this mess."

"Listen to me! If you touch him with even one finger, I'll let the whole world know what I learned about the sementals..." Rosie let the sentence dangle, unfinished.

"Don't listen to what she is saying. She is clearly in shock and in need of psychiatric assistance. The poor thing won't even be able to raise her own child," Bruna said, slowly looking around. "You are going to spend the rest of your life locked up, as I wisely suggested a long time ago. Finally, your mothers will listen to me," she added in a lower voice, meant to be heard only by Rosie.

"Bruna, I can start talking now. I can tell you exactly what happens at the Temple, where all the pure breeds go to have their children. Do you have kids, Colonel? Maybe you are interested in hearing a fascinating tale. Or maybe you already know... Do you, Colonel?" Rosie had managed to free herself from the publicist's tight grip on her arm.

"Rosie, you are playing a dangerous game," Bruna cautioned her.

"Am I, Bruna? Maybe you're the one who doesn't know about the incognito—"

"Stop there, Rosie. You don't know what you are doing."

"You won't intimidate me. I'll go with these men, and you'll let me take your car. As long as you don't come after me, I won't say a word." Rosie moved closer to Mauricio and put a hand on the gun still pressing against his skin. The colonel flinched at Rosie's gesture.

"Move the gun, now," Rosie said to the colonel, who was trying to decide whose orders to follow.

Mauricio could see from the colonel's indecision that she had no clue what Rosie was talking about. But Bruna did. *It's written all over your ugly face.*

"Bruna, I am not bluffing. Tell the colonel I'm dead serious," Rosie said, trying to press the gun away from Mauricio's body. The colonel was now looking anxiously at the publicist.

"Rosie, think for once in your life. Think for Heavens' sake! He's just a slave! Why do you want to ruin your life for... something less valuable than an animal?" Bruna was furious. She spat the words while walking closer to Rosie.

"Stay where you are. I think it's story time. Sit down and relax; it's going to take a while to explain everything." Rosie raised one outstretched hand, but the publicist wasn't impressed by the gesture; the woman simply stared at Rosie with an unreadable look on her face and then turned her head toward the colonel.

"Shoot her as well," Bruna commanded the colonel, who stared back in shock. The night became preternaturally silent and still.

"I don't think I understand—" the older woman said after a long pause, but Rosie interrupted her.

"You do realize that she can't get away with killing me without killing everybody else here." Rosie was talking directly to the colonel now. "She can't risk it. She can't have a full investigation with all of you alive. Sooner or later, someone could talk," she added when she saw the colonel's arm falter slightly. "She will ask you to kill all the guards, and then she is going to get rid of you. Maybe not tonight. Probably not tomorrow. She'll still need you to confirm her story, at least for a few months. But your days are numbered if you kill me. I am your life insurance policy. If you don't shoot me or the slaves, you have my promise that if anything happens to you, I am going to talk." She tried to reason with the colonel. Meanwhile, several guards had gathered around them and watched intently.

"Don't listen to her. I only want to protect the President from a scandal that could end her career," Bruna interjected.

"It's not just about my mother's career. You want to shut my mouth because what I know will destroy your precious Ginecean status quo. And you don't want that. You have influenced my mother's political decisions for so long that you can't lose it now. But you were in too much of a rush, Bruna. You shouldn't have asked the colonel to kill me. That was a mistake."

Mauricio looked around to see how many guards were there, waiting for an order.

"Do you think that any of you can get away with killing the President's daughter?" Rosie asked the closest guard. The woman looked away immediately.

"My mothers won't rest until they have discovered what happened to me," Rosie pressed her point.

"But you see, sweetheart, I'll be the one directing the operation," Bruna said.

"Exactly. Think—" Rosie put one finger on her temple and looked around to see the reaction on the other women's faces. "— think about what she just said. *She* will be the one supervising that nothing, absolutely nothing, comes out. And the only way to assure it is to make sure that nobody is left to contradict her." Rosie locked her eyes on the colonel.

Soft murmurs started to fill the silence.

"She's right. Colonel, she's right!" the woman standing guard over Captain Reece said. Another agreed loudly. The guards who didn't talk nodded nervously. The colonel slowly retracted her hand.

Mauricio started breathing again.

"You are making a huge mistake, Colonel," Bruna hissed and was going to say something else, but an idea crossed her mind and she acted on it before anybody could do anything to stop her. She attacked the guard who had just spoken, took her gun, and shot the captain. Then, before the guard could react, Bruna shot her as well.

What the—

"Now, who's next? You, Colonel? Or you, Rosie? Anyone going to argue with me now? No? I didn't think so. What I think is that the slave here took the gun from the heroic guard who was trying to save her captain. The slave shot them both and then, when he saw that there was no way out of it, he shot himself as well. Yes, that's how it went. You, Colonel, arrived just a second too late, but in time to save the rest of the troop. You, Rosie, will be too traumatized to be reacquainted with society. Your ticket for the Mental Illness Center has been ready for a while. I am not sure that you kept the baby, unfortunately. Actually, you were never pregnant. A therapy based on a series of electroshocks will eventually cure your memory. If you didn't die in the carnage tonight, of course. That's something I have yet to decide," she said without blinking once.

"I'll confess to every single crime you want to accuse me of, and I'll gladly die for something I never did if you leave Rosie and the baby alone." Mauricio was already on his knees. "I'll be your scapegoat. Just let her have a normal life."

"How dare you talk to me?" Bruna pointed the gun at him.

"You should listen to what the slave is proposing," one guard whispered.

"If the slave is accused of what happened here, we're all off the hook," another found the courage to add.

"He's a fugitive already, along with the other two. If we pin everything on him, nobody is going to investigate further. He'll be executed, and we're not going to reveal anything about tonight. It's in our interest to keep our mouths shut," the guard who had spoken first, who had been reassured by the other heads nodding in unison, added.

"Maybe you should at least consider what they are saying," the colonel said softly.

Please…

"Bruna, there must be another way out." Rosie looked exhausted; she fell to her knees so she was side-by-side with Mauricio.

"If that isn't a sweet sight. The precious brat where she should be: on her knees like a beggar. You don't deserve the exceptionally good luck you had at your birth. I think I'll go back to my former plan and kill you anyway. I deserve some satisfaction, after all. But maybe I'll get rid of someone else first. So, who's it going to be?" She brandished the gun this way and that. She finally decided on her target, and with a sick smile, she aimed at Rosie's belly.

CHAPTER 11

Mauricio acted out of pure instinct and threw Rosie away from the bullet's trajectory. At the same moment, the colonel fired her gun at Bruna. She collapsed on the ground, her eyes locked on the older woman with a surprised expression.

Mauricio stared in fascination at the whole scene. *Why is everyone moving so slowly? I can barely hear a thing.*

"Mauricio!" He heard Rosie calling him from far away. *Thank the Goddess Bruna didn't get you,* was his first thought when she came into view and saw that she was unharmed. *It's okay, everything is fine. You don't need to be worried anymore.* Then he followed the direction of her eyes and saw blood coming out of his midsection. *Oh...* The pain arrived several seconds later.

Rosie caught his head before he hit the ground and immediately applied pressure against the wound. "Somebody help me!" she screamed, tears streaming down her face. None of the women came closer, but Leander and Arias dragged themselves to Mauricio's side. They were barely conscious but tried to help.

Nobody heard the third vehicle coming. It stopped by the fugitives' car with the tires sending up fumes. The strident sound and the acrid smell elicited a mild interest in the guards, who were closer to the car. Only when a door opened and then slapped back in place with a fury did the colonel turn around. "Madame President," she greeted the imposing shadow, her voice nervous.

"Mom?" Rosie raised one hand to screen her eyes from the high beams.

Darya Layan, the President of Ginecea, here. What an honor. Mauricio, in his pain-induced haze, almost found the situation funny. There was blood everywhere, and the colonel was cowering under the President's darting eyes.

"Rosie?" the President bellowed when she saw her. "What did they do to you?" she asked horrified, once closer.

Mauricio felt Rosie's body become rigid when her mother went to touch her. She had turned to look at him while the other woman was trying to get her attention. Then she was torn from him.

"What happened to her?" the President screamed to anybody who would answer her question. She gathered a bloodied Rosie in her lap and cradled her. In a few seconds, her hands and her clothes were smeared in blood, too. "Rosie, where are you wounded?" she asked.

Mauricio saw two women approaching and recognized an out-of-breath Guen, who took a good look at Rosie and then nodded at her.

"Rosie! Oh my Heavens, honey. So much blood!" the other woman cried.

"Rina! I told you to wait in the car," Darya Layan said.

Rosie disappeared under her second mother's suffocating embrace.

"The First Lady was too worried," Guen explained to the President and then mouthed to Mauricio, "Everything is going to be okay now." She then crouched beside him to check his pulse.

"I'm not wounded. I don't have a scratch on me. The men did nothing to me," Rosie finally answered her mother's question. "Bruna ordered the colonel to kill me."

"I—" The President stared at her daughter.

"Mom, this man needs a doctor, immediately," Rosie said and then turned toward Guen and lowered her voice, "He looks paler than he did a moment ago."

"What are you talking about?" the President asked.

"Rosie, we have wounded women here that need medical attention," Rina said, looking at the captain and at the other guard lying on the ground.

"They don't need anything anymore," Rosie impatiently said.

Her mother, Rina, opened her mouth to intervene, but her wife spoke first. "Maybe they don't, but Bruna does." The President looked at Rosie, shocked.

"She killed them. She doesn't deserve to live. You have to call the doctor for *this* man. Please, we are wasting time he doesn't have." Rosie was getting anxious. "I don't care what you want to do with Bruna; she can wait, but he can't." Rosie took Mauricio's hand in hers.

Both of her mothers gasped in horror at the sight of their daughter touching a man.

"Rosie? What is it happening here?" Rina asked when it was clear that Darya was too shocked to talk.

"What's happening?" Rosie repeated. "What's happening, you ask me? An innocent human being is bleeding to death before your eyes, and you are doing nothing."

"A slave's life isn't worth our bother," Darya answered.

Mauricio was trying to remain awake, but it was getting hard to breathe.

"Rosie, something must be done immediately," Arias said.

"Moms! I'll never forgive you if you don't try to save his life." Rosie didn't turn to see their reaction. "Mauricio, I love you."

"I love you," he said through his blurred vision, happiness spreading through his cold body.

She leaned closer and brushed his forehead with her lips and then moved toward his mouth.

Mauricio's heart somersaulted in his chest a second time. Not so long ago, the proximity of her mouth to his had elicited a similar reaction in his body. *If anything else, you're going to kill me for sure.* His lips curved up.

A scream stopped her from getting any closer. Rosie's protective shadow moved away, and he felt lost.

"Rosie! Move away from the slave." Darya was shaking. She raised her hand to slap her daughter, but Rina stopped her before she could hit Rosie.

"The doctor is on her way. I called her as soon as we arrived," Guen said to Rosie, and then she turned to face her mothers. "This semental is too precious. Tarin can't afford to lose a good specimen without reason."

"This semental is worth nothing, and I have already signed his death sentence." Darya Layan, the President of Ginecea once again, confronted Guen with a cold stare.

"I apologize, Madame President, I didn't know about your orders," Guen lied, lowering her head.

At the same time, Bruna thrashed around, moaning loudly, and the Layans hurried to her side.

"I'll be right back," Guen whispered to Rosie and went to the colonel's car, only to come back a few seconds later with a briefcase. "Move aside for a moment. Let me see if there's something I can use from this first aid kit."

Don't leave me alone. Mauricio was glad for Rosie's hands caressing his throbbing temples. *I'm so tired.* His eyes weren't working properly, red spots were dancing where Guen's face should have been.

"He needs blood," Guen said.

Mauricio distractedly observed the woman raising his shirt to expose the wound. *I don't feel a thing. Why don't I feel anything?* He thought while Guen touched his abdomen.

"I'm a universal donor. I'll give it to him," Rosie proposed.

No, you won't.

Guen slowly shook her head and said, "You're pregnant."

"You must be kidding!" The President's voice came from behind Guen. She and her wife stood a few feet from them, staring in horror at their daughter. "You can't donate blood in your state! And... to a slave. Are you completely insane?" Darya stomped toward Rosie, but Rina took her arm.

"Think of your baby." Rina kept Darya from moving any farther.

"I am," Rosie muttered under her breath.

Guen raised an eyebrow and gave Rosie a pointed look.

"For Heavens' sake, what are you talking about?" Darya freed herself from her wife's hold.

"What is she talking about?" Rina asked Guen.

Bruna cried and compelled the Layans' full attention once more.

"Rosie, you should calm down." Guen gently touched Rosie's forearm and then bent her head to whisper, "I don't think your mothers know anything about what you are saying, and I don't think it's a good idea to talk before all these other women."

Listen to her.

"You know?" Rosie asked.

"If I understood what you were trying to say, I know." Guen looked behind her shoulders at the President, who was leaning over a motionless Bruna.

"The incognito the Priestess used to make me conceive my baby—" Rosie was interrupted by Guen's hand over her mouth.

"Then, I know," Guen whispered and took away her hand. "Maintain your calm now, and we'll find a way to save the three of them."

"I'll try—" Rosie looked down at Mauricio. Then she tilted her head toward Guen. "How did you manage to get away with helping me?" she asked, darting a glance beyond them where the other women were.

"Nobody saw me, and when the electricity came back, I was back behind my desk at the control room. As soon as the distress call arrived, I volunteered to escort your mothers."

"Doctor's here," one of the guards called.

"I'll go talk to her," Guen said, already walking to meet the doctor.

Mauricio watched as Guen and the doctor were directed toward Bruna by Rina. Rosie stood up, ready to make a scene. "It's okay," he said, trying to raise his arm to touch her. *There's nothing else you can do for me.*

Rosie didn't seem to hear him, her eyes looking at something shiny on the ground. "I need help! I'm bleeding," she screamed and rolled down as if in pain.

That woke Mauricio's addled brain. "Rosie?" Before he could articulate something more, she was back at his side holding a dark, elongated shape in her hand.

Guen and the doctor ran to see what was happening to her. The doctor promptly went to move Rosie away from Mauricio.

"Don't even think about it," Rosie growled, aiming a rifle at the doctor. "Now, you'll take a look at him."

The doctor looked at Rosie with a stupefied expression, but she didn't say anything.

"And, you'll tell my mothers that everything is under control here."

"Rosie is fine, just a scratch. Keep applying pressure on Bruna's wound," the doctor yelled, stopping the Layans in their steps. "You can lower that rifle now, if you want me to check on this slave."

Rosie relaxed her grip on the weapon and pointed it at the ground. The doctor leaned toward Mauricio, looked at him, and touched his chest. When he didn't react to the probing, she shook her head.

Is bad this time, isn't it?

"What is it?" Rosie asked.

"There isn't time to go back to the infirmary." The doctor raised her eyes to look at Guen.

I guessed so myself.

"Okay, let's do what we can here." Guen stood up and called one of the guards.

It's colder all of a sudden.

"He's shivering a lot," Rosie said.

Mauricio felt her hands protectively resting on his shoulders, and he smiled. *Leave us alone for a moment.*

"I need help clearing a space where I can clean the slave's wound and remove the bullet. I am not sure if it will be enough," the doctor said.

"She'll help me clear the space." Guen pointed at the guard, "And, you, go with the doctor, see if she needs anything else," she added, looking at Rosie.

"I am not leaving him."

Please, stay. I need to tell you something...

"Would you rather dig a grave for him? Every hand is needed, and we don't have a nurse," Guen said, and the doctor nodded.

"I'll be right back," she answered.

Without Rosie holding him, Mauricio felt colder while the pain made him shiver and sweat. He closed his eyes and hoped to faint, but remained awake. A few feet from him, out of earshot from the other women, the President and the colonel were having an animated discussion. When Guen directed the guard toward them, the two women moved closer to Mauricio.

Don't mind me.

"Madame President, it seems that your daughter is in possession of information that is potentially dangerous for the Ginecean society," the colonel said. "I don't know exactly what it is that scared your publicist, but she was ready to kill all of us to keep it a secret. This slave took the bullet meant for your daughter. Although his life is expendable, it seems that your daughter has formed a bond of some sort with him. And I am worried about two things…"

"Which are?"

That she's a decent human being for starters?

"The first is that we don't know exactly what secret Rosie is keeping, and she was adamant about using that knowledge to save these men. The second is that the guards have seen the way Rosie interacted with this slave, and I can't guarantee that they will keep their mouths shut. Perversion is the most horrible brand. Even if she doesn't say what she knows, she has already proclaimed that she wants to leave with these men. Your family, and your career, will be ruined by the scandal." The colonel spoke slowly.

Oh, that would be too bad, I suppose.

"And being so… what do you suggest?" Darya asked.

"I suggest letting the doctor save the slave–" the colonel started.

I like that. Mauricio's hopes were kindled for the briefest of moments.

"I won't listen to this. Even if he did save my daughter!" the President exclaimed.

"He did—"

"He is just another worthless slave, for Heavens' sake."

"I agree with you…"

"But?"

"But, if the slave dies, and your daughter thinks that we haven't tried everything possible, who knows how she would react. She seems… well… deranged, with all due respect." The colonel made an apologetic expression and raised her hands.

"You have my permission to talk."

"Tell your daughter you'll let the doctor save the slave, with the conditions that she won't follow him anywhere, and that she'll tell you what she knows in private," the colonel finished.

"Why are you doing this? Why are you trying to help me?"

"Because it's my job, and I voted for you," the colonel answered.

"I have never thought that one day I would have to confront something… like this." The President of Ginecea turned her face slightly toward Mauricio, and he saw the anger in her face.

"She'll be fine when the baby is born. Marry her off right away," the colonel said, looking at Rosie coming back with the doctor. Guen followed a second later, accompanied by two guards.

No! He was dying, but the idea of her married to someone else was too painful to bear.

"Bring him here," Guen commanded the guards.

Careful, it hurts! Mauricio hated the cruel hands that hauled him onto the blanket spread over the cleared patch. Rosie was immediately by his side, and she kept touching him while the doctor cut his shirt down the front. He was in tremendous pain, and his body was going into shock. He heard Rosie crying.

"I'm sorry for everything," he said to her. *You deserved so much better.*

"I'm not going to lose you! Do you hear me?" Rosie said.

"Mistress, if you don't calm down, I'll have to give you a sedative, and I'd rather avoid that," the doctor said.

"Is he going to make it?" Rosie asked, gently cushioning his head on her belly.

Mauricio thought he could hear a softer set of heartbeats. A sentiment akin to pure joy invaded him. "Can you feel that?" he asked, or he thought had asked.

"It's worse than I thought; I can't see where the bullet is lodged," the doctor answered.

"Is he going to make it?" Rosie repeated, her voice louder.

"Only if he can make it back to Tarin."

"We must go, then." Rosie's tears were washing Mauricio's face.

Don't cry. "It's okay." Everybody was talking at the same time, and his voice wasn't strong enough to cut through the noise.

The doctor shook her head. "He needs blood, now."

"I'll give him my blood," Rosie announced, and the President swore.

"Is anybody else a universal donor?" Darya's voice carried toward the rest of the group. The guards were waiting for orders and had spontaneously moved to stand together. They heard the questions, but shook their heads or answered with murmured *no's.* "Of course."

Of course, he thought at the same time as the President.

"I won't let him die. I can save him, and you won't stop me." Rosie cradled Mauricio in her lap, while directing the rifle against the rest of the women.

A collective gasp was followed by a long moment of silence.

"Come here, now!" the President called her daughter.

"You won't change my mind, and I'm not a minor. I will use all I know against you, if necessary," Rosie said, leaning over Mauricio's body. "I'm not leaving him alone again."

You should think about that... I don't think I've got much longer.

Mauricio saw the look in the President's eyes and feared the worst for Rosie. He tried to talk, but couldn't move his lips.

After another long pause, the President slowly walked toward her daughter and said, "I'm willing to consider saving this slave's life if you accept my proposition." The woman was now crouched beside Rosie, a few inches from his face, and Mauricio saw the cruel light in her eyes. He shivered again.

"I'm listening," Rosie said.

Don't. I won't survive the night, anyway. Mauricio moaned.

"If you donate your blood, you could lose your baby. It's too dangerous; I won't permit it." Darya let the statement sink in.

I won't permit that, either. He found it darkly amusing that he had agreed with the woman several times already.

"This is your idea of a proposition?"

"Let's go back to Tarin, where the doctor can find some blood for this slave."

"You're wasting time he doesn't have." Rosie moved the rifle in a circular motion, making several guards jump away. "Doctor, what are you waiting for?"

"Bruna is a universal donor," Guen said, emerging from the shadows. "It says so on this medallion." She showed it to the President, who took it from her hands and stormed away.

Mauricio saw Darya Layan and her wife talk to the colonel, while Rosie kept caressing him. He was slipping in and out of consciousness and couldn't feel much anymore. His eyes were too heavy, and he closed them for a moment.

He was startled by the sound of animated conversation. There was something wrong; Rosie's hands weren't on him, spreading her warmth over his frozen body. *Where are you?* At some point she must have left. In the peaceful quiet of the darkness, he heard her cry, but couldn't see where she was.

"But I'm not coming back with you. I want to live my life with him." She was talking to someone.

Oh, Rosie... I would've loved that. You, me, and our baby girl.

"I'm afraid that is not negotiable. It's either black or white. You decide," Darya said.

"You can't do this to me," Rosie was sobbing.

Don't cry for me; it doesn't matter. It' so peaceful now... I love you.

"*I can.* You're pregnant, and since you aren't married, I have jurisdiction over your health in case you are incapacitated. And as of this moment, you are." This time Rina spoke.

"Mom, please..."

"I told you; I'll let the slave have a transfusion from Bruna, only if you promise that this madness ends now."

What— Mauricio wasn't sure about anything anymore, and the voices were fading into a barely coherent mumble.

"One day, you'll thank us."

"We're losing the slave," the doctor announced.

"You can save him, Rosie," Darya pressed her point.

"Any moment now."

"I'll stay with you," Rosie capitulated.

CHAPTER 12

Mauricio looked at the sun lowering toward the horizon and then rearranged the new stone sculpture he had been creating for the last six months. The structure had grown in height more than in width and now resembled a willowy ghost of an idea Mauricio once had. He added a grey pebble and removed two white rocks. He looked at his creation and was satisfied by what he saw.

"Is that all for today, Priest?" a young boy named Lucas asked him.

"Yes, I guess so." He had been working on the stone sculptures for a while now and the landscape ahead of him was dotted with dozens of them.

"They are pretty," Lucas said. He had started his own small masterpiece and was now comparing his work to the Priest's.

"Yours is beautiful, too." Mauricio gazed at the boy's pile of pebbles.

"Does it have a soul, yet?" Lucas asked, worried.

"When you thought of it, you put the soul inside your sculpture." Mauricio patted the boy's head in affection. "Let's go to the Caves. Your mom and dad will be worried by the time we get there." Mauricio stood up and started walking. Lucas trotted graciously behind him. The boy was curious about the Priest's life and normally asked lots of questions, but today he was less chatty than usual.

"You are very pensive. Is there anything bothering you?" Mauricio asked when he couldn't stand the silence anymore. He loved kids because they coaxed him to talk.

"I have been thinking about you," Lucas started and then paused, slightly embarrassed.

"Have you now?"

"Yes, you're always alone, and I worry about you," Lucas finished all in one breath.

"I have lots of friends," Mauricio answered.

"Yes, it's true, but you live alone. Nobody keeps you company when you're in your house," Lucas countered.

"You know why I'm called the Priest?" Mauricio had this conversation at least once a year. It never failed to please him how kids could be so affectionate and spontaneous. And they had the naïve impudence to ask the questions adults whispered behind his back.

"You told me, but it doesn't make any sense. Why do you want to be alone?" Lucas was looking at him as if he had sprouted another set of eyes. Lucas' life was surrounded by people who loved him and cared for him.

"I'm waiting for someone." Mauricio smiled at his own words. Ten years later and still he came out every morning to gaze at the desert to see if Rosie was coming.

"Yeah, right," Lucas snorted and then turned an even redder shade than before. "Sorry, I didn't mean to offend you…"

"No offense taken. You're a good boy." Mauricio put a hand on his shoulder and applied the slightest pressure to reassure the boy he wasn't mad at him.

"What if your companion never comes?" Lucas didn't want to let it go now that he'd had the courage to broach the subject.

"Then I'll have my memories to keep me company." Mauricio smiled again.

He could still see her, ten years later. Rosie smiling at him and promising that she was going to reach for him as soon as she had the baby. Their precious little girl. One of the last things Rosie said to him was, "I will name our baby after you." As she reached through the bars to brush his fingers.

Rosie had managed to save his life, but there were consequences to pay. As soon as his health improved, he was transferred to the maximum-security wing. He spent his days anchored to the wall with a short chain that got even shorter when his guard caught Rosie holding his outstretched hands. Afterwards, any time she came to visit him, the guard locked his collar to a hook on the wall so that he couldn't move at all. Brushing fingertips became the only physical contact allowed them and the strain on his muscles was unbearable after several minutes of keeping the stance, yet he never uttered a word about it. He never got to see Rosie's belly grow, and he never discovered how she managed to free him in the end. Ten years were long enough for him to conjure a few theories, but he never knew for sure what happened. Guen accompanied Rosie the time she shared her plans for the baby's name. He hadn't seen the woman since that fateful night. He was happy to see her and even more so when she entered his cell and unlocked him.

"You have a whole hour. Make it count," Guen said with a wistful tone. Without another word, she deactivated his collar and left.

Rosie was beautiful that day, but she was also sad. Mauricio had looked at her in devotion from his cell, uncertain of what he was allowed to do. She walked inside and said, "Let's go for a stroll. The night is beautiful outside."

He followed Rosie, his fingers brushing hers, looking at her profile as if it were the first time he had laid eyes on her. She smiled every time their sideways glances met, but kept walking in complete silence. He didn't ask how this opportunity was even possible. He didn't want to waste the little time they had been given. He was absolutely mesmerized by the fact that they were walking together and that he could freely touch her hand. Rosie led the way outside. They didn't meet any guards and the door to the fields was already open. The cold air chilled his skin and made him shiver, but he was used to pain, and her presence was the only salve he needed for his mangled body. He was skin and bones, and his muscles weren't working properly, so he staggered several times on the uneven ground. But Rosie was there to help him, and he didn't fall. They walked past the cafeteria and stopped at a bench he hadn't noticed before.

"Sit beside me," Rosie said, patting the stone bench. Mauricio sat, and by the moonlight, he saw that she was crying. He reached for her face and wiped her tears with a soft caress. He had never been so close to her, fully awake, and his heart was pounding and his ears ringing.

"I love you," he whispered to her.

"I love you," she said back, her voice tinged with a heartbreaking sweetness, her bright eyes looking at him with an intensity that made him shiver, her hands seeking his. "I've never thought I could feel for someone the way I feel for you. I want you to remember this. I'll always love you."

"Rosie, my Rosie…" It was difficult to look at her and talk at the same time. He wanted to take her in his arms, but he didn't move; her mere presence had him frozen. *You're my Goddess.*

"You know what I'd like to do now?" she asked, freeing him from the spell.

"No, what would you like to do?" Mauricio smiled, remembering their previous conversations started with the same question.

"I'd like for us to have a date."

"A date?" He didn't know what she was talking about.

"Yes, like normal couples do."

"What do you do in a date?"

"You go out—" She lowered her eyes for a moment.

"We are out." He smiled at her. "What else?"

"People talk about their lives, what they like to do, about their youth, their pets…"

"What did you like to do when you were a kid?"

"Do you want to hear about that?" Rosie asked with the softest voice.

"Yes, please."

Mauricio still remembered every single word she had spoken ten years earlier. He also remembered the way her intonation sounded different from the way the other women talked. She talked as if she was singing and pronounced every letter as if it mattered. He also remembered how her hands waved through the air while she was saying something about her childhood. He didn't have anything pleasant to tell her about him, so he simply listened, enchanted by her grace. Mauricio had been happy, truly happy, during that hour.

"Would you like to build a stone sculpture with me?" she asked after having told him about her summers spent with her grandmothers at a resort by the sea.

"I don't know what it is," he answered.

Rosie explained to him what a stone sculpture was, while looking for rocks of different sizes.

"I like the smooth stones you can find on the shore," she said, giving him a pile of small rocks. "I have been building stone sculptures as long as I can remember. Every little rock is a memory."

They worked balancing three stones, one on top of the other, until she stopped his hand. "This is it. It's done. It's perfect."

Mauricio looked at the rocks piled in a pyramid shape, and thought it was beautiful.

"This is you," she said, touching the biggest rock sitting on the bottom. "This is me, and the small one on top is our Maurice."

Rosie then told him about that one time when, looking for the perfect stone, she had climbed a wet rock wall and fell. "Guen is coming for you," she said suddenly, after showing him the healed wound on her right knee.

"She'll go with you and you'll both be safe, far away from here." Rosie's tears were hurting him, but he understood that she didn't want him to ask anything. "You'll be free, and you'll never have to come back here." She continued pressing his hand on her heart. Mauricio could still remember how warm and alive she had felt under his fingers. Sometimes at night, when he missed her the most, he liked to imagine the texture of her skin on his.

"You'll have a beautiful life," Rosie said.

"But I want to be with you." Mauricio hated hearing the sadness in her voice. "I'm not going anywhere without you," he said, even though he knew he was talking nonsense. There wasn't any life together for them. If he wanted to see her, even through bars, it meant going back to his cell, hoping that Rosie's mothers would let her continue visiting.

"I feared so…"

"I prefer to go back if it's the only way to see you," Mauricio said truthfully. He didn't care to be free that much. He didn't even know what it felt like.

"You don't have to go back. I—" Rosie paused for few seconds, collecting her words. "—will reach you. When the baby is born, I'll leave everything behind and I'll come to live with you."

Mauricio didn't say anything, but Rosie understood his silent question and answered immediately. "I can't come with you right now, because the baby is not well. No—" She saw the panic in his face and hurried to reassure him. "—no, don't worry. I'll take good care of our daughter and when she is strong enough, we'll reach you."

"I love you," Mauricio said again, feeling that the hour had already expired, and he had so many things he wanted to tell her. "I have something for you… a gift."

"You have a gift for me?" Rosie's eyes were bright with tears, already.

"I want to give you something." He took her hands in his. "It means a lot to me, and after what you have told me tonight, it's the perfect gift for you."

"What is it?" Rosie asked before opening her hands to see what was inside them.

"My freedom," he answered.

"It's beautiful." She slowly caressed the smooth surface of the pebble Mauricio had given her.

"I picked it up from the ground the first time I set foot outside. I kept it on me this whole time; you can build a sculpture with it, if you want."

"Thank you… this is the most beautiful gift I have ever received. I'll never part from it." Rosie couldn't contain her emotions anymore. "You are the love of my life." She leaned ever so slowly and raised her lips to meet his.

Mauricio had never been kissed before. The softness of her mouth met his cracked skin and restored him fully. He felt the air leaving her body and it smelled sweet. His arms went around her, embracing her tiny body, and she said his name. It sounded pure.

To this day, he never let anyone call him Mauricio again. Nobody else had that right. It was hers. He was Mauricio only for Rosie, for the rest of the City of Men, he was simply the Priest.

"Priest?" Lucas asked with a worried face, and Mauricio came back from the past.

"Yes, Lucas." Everybody knew that his mind tended to wander aimlessly, but only the kids complained about it. The adults were too intimidated by his persona.

"You haven't answered my question about what you are going to teach tomorrow." Lucas was the smartest kid in his class; he always had an abundance of questions when he entered the classroom each morning.

"Tomorrow, we are going to study the Ethical Rights on which our City of Men is based," Mauricio said, in his best formal tone. He loved that lesson. He couldn't wait for the right time of the year when he taught about their constitution. Normally, Guen and Arias made an appearance for the occasion; otherwise, they preferred to stay at the Sanctuary with their daughter, Cordelia. Even in the City of Men, where everybody was free, married couples of different genders weren't widely accepted. Mauricio was still fighting that battle and it pained him that his friends weren't integrated inside the city they had helped build. But at least they lived close to the city, still outside its borders, but close enough.

Compared to Lucas' home, Guen and Arias' Sanctuary was just around the corner. When he was born, Lucas' parents had decided to move to the Caves, a big natural compound with a system of caves—hence the name—and springs. They weren't the only ones there; other families who didn't feel safe in the City of Men had joined them. Nobody knew exactly how many families were there. They remained separated, but at least Mauricio had convinced the Cavers to send the kids to school. Everybody trusted the Priest's words. He had promised that the kids would be safe with him, and so they were.

While walking Lucas safely home, he wondered, as he often did when he was with kids around ten years old, how his daughter was doing. Maurice was ten now, and he imagined her as a small replica of his beloved Rosie. He pictured Maurice with chestnut hair, hazel eyes, and maybe freckles on her nose. She would be funny, smart, and talk with her mother's lilting accent. Mauricio had never stopped waiting for Rosie, even if he knew deep inside what she had bargained that night to give him freedom: Rosie had given up her own.

He had kept in contact with Ginecea, and he had read with tears in his eyes of the ecstatic news about the First Daughter's wedding. He had built a web of spies in all the slaves' facilities, and they were good at reporting anything he asked. And he had asked to know anything regarding the First family, anything at all. He had a box full of clippings from magazines that he opened every night before going to bed. There weren't many pictures of Rosie after she had married; she and her wife conducted a photographer-shy life somewhere on the marine coast, away from the bright lights of Ginecea. If Rosie's pictures were few, Maurice's were none. Rosie had never given permission to snap photos of the baby. And so Mauricio had to imagine what his daughter looked like, but he knew about her through what the press wrote. He knew that she was a good student, that she was kind to her mothers, and that she liked to visit the First House. He knew she took ballet lessons and that her dream was to become the youngest President of Ginecea one day.

He was proud of his Maurice and would have given anything to talk to her. *One step at the time,* he used to remind himself when he had bouts of melancholy. Every time he freed a slave, it was a step closer to a better Ginecea. A Ginecea where slavery was illegal. One day, men and women would live together, free to love whomever they wanted. But, it was too much to ask in a single generation. He knew that. It would take decades to change current society, but someone had to start it. Someone had to take the first step toward the realization of such a dream.

He had taken that first heavy step, and with that step, he had laid the foundation for a better world; he had also destroyed any chance to see Rosie and his daughter again. He hadn't known that when he started his journey of exile and self-preservation he would create a place where dreams could finally be dreamed. He hadn't realized that because he was too busy living for the first time in his life. The first nucleus of the City of Men had been created by three desperate fugitives who had nothing to lose and a courageous woman who had nothing to gain by staying with them.

"Yes?" Mauricio looked down at Lucas, pointing at his midsection with a laughing smile.

"It has been ringing for more than five minutes." The boy couldn't help to be amused by the Priest's ability of losing track of reality.

Mauricio followed the boy's finger and saw his cell phone illuminated. He smiled at Lucas and opened the battered phone.

"Leander?" Mauricio acknowledged the other man's easily recognizable voice.

"You're late." Leander was one of the few, along with Guen and Arias, who wouldn't call him Priest. But Leander also avoided, if possible, calling him Mauricio, since he knew that name was painful for his friend to hear.

"I need to escort an important person to his home first," Mauricio answered, winking at Lucas, whose smile widened.

"Say hi to Lucas for me. Then hurry back to the well." Leander had the happiest tone.

"Is it working?" Mauricio asked.

"Yes, we're waiting for you to do things officially." Leander's voice was light. After so many months, almost a full year of working double shifts, the new well was ready to give potable water to the growing population of the City of Men. They had managed ten years with several small wells that didn't reach deep enough, but had produced an adequate amount of rationed water for the first group of citizens. At the beginning, it had been difficult to find aquifers. They didn't have any instrument to locate water, only a strong will to survive. They had become thieves by necessity. They had only stolen what they needed from the women's facilities under Mauricio's direct orders.

"It's bad enough we can't even beg for what we need the most, but we will not, under any circumstances, succumb to the temptation of taking what is superfluous. We will educate ourselves, and we will thrive, thanks to our labor. We will go to bed every night knowing that we did our best with what we have been dealt. Little or much. And we will wake up every morning with the certainty that what we do is going to make a difference." Leander had written down what was universally known as the Priest's first speech. The nickname had come soon after, when people realized that, while everybody was looking for their soulmates, he simply thought about building the foundation for what would one day become the City of Men. Mauricio's asceticism, his gift with words, his sharp mind, and most of all, his devotion to the mission of creating a better world for everybody, had granted him the title Priest.

Mauricio had always found his nickname ironic. It was the male counterpart for the word "Priestess," and he wanted nothing to do with her, not even by a distant phonetic connotation. She was everything that was wrong with Ginecea, and whereas she had built her power on a castle of lies and prevarications against one race, Mauricio wanted to free peoples' minds and teach them the truth. He didn't want power; he didn't like that the desert community of fugitive men and rejected women looked at him as their leader. He only wanted to have a family. Like Guen and Arias. Like Lucas and his parents. Like Leander and Julius. He wanted love, like everybody else.

Instead, he went to his apartment alone every night, as Lucas had pointed out. He always had a meal on the table. The community cared for him, and he didn't need anything in terms of food, clothing, or shelter. But he longed for the family that would never be and rarely accepted invitations to share his free time with others. It was too painful to watch parents interact with their kids or couples trying to hide their affection for fear of wounding him. What was left for him was to dedicate his celibate and indefatigable mind to the betterment of their society.

A communal well had been his pet project for some time now. He had needed new geology texts to get an idea about what was necessary to drill deeper than they had before. A particularly thankful group of ex-slaves had helped him with the logistics of getting the texts. They had stolen the books for him from Sundial, a facility that was dangerously close to their dwelling. He had studied the texts every night until his brain could take no more, and finally, he had come out with a feasible plan. Finding the perfect spot had been equally strenuous, but Mauricio loved the challenges that filled his time and his mind with positive energy. And now it was finally done. Water would be available for everybody at least once a day. It was a great step forward for the City of Men. It was the turning point that Mauricio had been waiting for. Finally, they could start plowing fields large enough to supply food for the whole community. Nothing fancy at first, just basic starches and grains.

"I'll come as soon as I drop off Lucas." Mauricio smiled and then added, "Thanks, Leander."

"For?" Leander's voice was muffled by the sound of cheering people.

"For being with me from the beginning," Mauricio said, remembering the night a young man had risked everything to help him escape.

"I got the best part out of the deal," Leander answered with sincerity and ended the conversation before Mauricio could reply. Leander always felt guilty when talking with him. As if Mauricio had gotten the short end of the stick, while he had won the jackpot. Over the years, the sentiment had become ingrained in their friendship, like a ghost haunting their happy moments. Mauricio had tried to explain to Leander that he was happy for him and that he deserved every moment of joy he had so strenuously worked for. The Priest had celebrated Leander and Julius' union, and he was also the godfather of Ariane, the orphan girl they had adopted. But no amount of reassurance on Mauricio's end could make Leander feel any better.

"And if you find someone whom you love even more?" Lucas asked after some woolgathering of his own. It seemed that while Mauricio was talking to Leander, the boy had kept thinking about the Priest's solitude.

"I discovered long ago that I'm a man who has been blessed with one true love."

"But you could try to live with someone and maybe, after a while, discover that this person is nice. Maybe even nicer than the other one you are always thinking of." Lucas had put a few thoughts together about fixing the Priest's lonely life.

Mauricio was sure that the kid had also written down a few possible names. "Well, I see your point... but it wouldn't be fair for this person you have in mind."

"Why not? He is nice enough!" Lucas said with great conviction.

"I am sure that he is more than nice. But I am also sure that he is someone else's soulmate, and as you can understand, it would be a disgrace if he got stuck with me when he could be with someone he could love with all his heart. Don't you agree with me?" Mauricio patiently explained.

"Yes, but..." Lucas was pouting now.

"Don't you want for me the same that your mom and dad have?" Mauricio asked softly.

"Of course I want that!" Lucas seemed surprised by the Priest's question.

"Then I can't simply share my life with someone I know isn't my true love." Mauricio was glad to see the entry to the Caves looming ahead of them. Lucas was in the mood to keep going for hours, and he simply wasn't. "You'll see. One day it will make absolute sense." Mauricio rested his arm on the kid's shoulder.

"I hope you're right." Lucas wasn't convinced.

"I see your mom." Mauricio waved his hand in the direction of a young woman waiting for them just inside the entry of the Caves' system.

"Thanks!" She waved back.

"See you tomorrow." Lucas hugged the Priest before running toward his mom's outstretched hands.

Mauricio stayed there a few seconds more, looking at the maternal scene. His eyes filled with tears, but he didn't avert them from the loving embrace of mother and son. It was beautiful, and he couldn't have enough of it, even if he was supposed to hurry back. When, with a last salute, Lucas disappeared inside the entry, Mauricio finally turned around and started walking briskly toward the fields. Leander and the well crew were waiting for him to pump the first bucket of water. Later, the entire community was going to celebrate in the central area that constituted the heart of the City of Men. He was proud of the work his men and women had done to transform an arid patch of desert into something worth fighting for. They reclaimed life where none was to be had. They shaped the rocks and the sand into something that they could call their own.

The City of Men was being built, one rock at a time, upon a design Mauricio had sketched in the sand one morning after a long, sleepless night. He had imagined a rocky tower, impossible to distinguish from the rest of the desert, with a hollow inside, full of colors. Mauricio wanted to give its citizens the freedom to express their personalities. He wanted to see colors and flowers and plants and anything else pleasing to the eyes. He wanted a place where everybody could be happy. Men and women would eventually live under the same roof in peace and harmony. Unfortunately, ten years weren't enough to forget about slavery, torture, and humiliation. But under the Priest's legislation, every act of violence against any other human being was treated as the most heinous crime and was dealt with accordingly. It had pained him greatly when he had to condemn to death by exile the two men who had killed Ariane's mother. And he hadn't rejoiced when the men's bones had been found one month later, but it had been the right message to send.

Nowadays, the other problem the City of Men was facing was the high infant and maternal mortality rate. Mauricio had asked for medical texts, and they came, along with a few highly needed supplies, from the same facility that had *generously lent* the geology texts. He had spent more sleepless nights studying female physiology, and he had been able to save a few lives, but babies were still dying. It pained him to think about it. *At least clean water is no longer a problem*, Mauricio reminded himself. It felt good to know that every action counted for something; he wasn't propagating a race of slaves for the sake of pure breeds anymore. He walked toward the fields, thinking of all the improvements he had helped create, and he felt at peace with the universe. He was doing the best with what life had given him.

Even though he would have gone back to his cell to remain
with Rosie that night, ten years ago, he knew now that it would
have been selfish. His community had been looking to him for
guidance so long; he didn't know any other life. Sometimes, when
he was tired and lonelier than usual, he entertained the idea that
someone else could have stepped up to lead. Someone had to
sacrifice his or her life and take the first step. So, who better than
him? He'd never had a chance to live a normal life with Rosie,
while everybody else could still have a shot at happiness. He had
fallen in love with the President's daughter. He, Mauricio, the ex-
slave, the former semental, now the Priest, leader of a community
that was everything the Ginecean government was against, would
have never had a future with Rosie under any circumstance.

The fields stretched ahead of him, not the magnificent sight of
the Tarin's orchards, but something wondrous, nevertheless. There
was no river winding around at the edge of the horizon, no
kaleidoscope of colors arranged by shades. The City of Men's
fields were small and scattered to better use the rocky soil, and at
the moment, they were colorless. Still, for all their ugliness and
lack of visible appeal, those meager fields were his dream come
true. Mauricio felt proud of everything his life had turned out to be
and even prouder of the people he'd had the good fortune to share
his journey with. One of them was waving at him impatiently from
the far side of the fields.

"Coming," Mauricio muttered under his breath and hurried
toward Leander and the rest of the crew. They looked exhausted.
They were covered in red dirt from head to worn-out boots, but
they were laughing and playing around with something that looked
like a crude attempt at a soccer ball. They were mostly men, young
in age and drunk with the idea of freedom. Some of them had just
been rescued and they were dizzy with happiness. The others,
veterans of the City of Men, were reminded by the new arrivals of
the fact that life for a man in Ginecea could be very different. The
women were still rare, and the few of them here were all fathered.
No pure breed, with the exception of Guen, could have accepted
the libertarian philosophy that was at the center of the City of

Men's community. Or the fact that owning slaves was illegal in Mauricio's world.

"Finally!" Leander ran toward Mauricio, tired of waiting for him.

"The boys want to start celebrating, and so do I." Julius came running after his husband.

"So, what are you waiting for?" Mauricio asked with a grin.

The men gathered around the Priest and started chanting his name, and one of the younger boys gave him a tin bucket.

"This is the beginning of something good for us, and all of you are responsible for making it a reality. Look at those fields and imagine what we will harvest next spring. Our kids will have nutritious food on their plates. Our life is going to change, and we have you to thank." The Priest spoke and everybody listened. Mauricio was still surprised that, when he talked, people stopped to commit to memory everything he said. He didn't like it in the beginning. He was still too much of a slave mentally to think of himself as worthy. Then he had relaxed and accepted that he had something other people didn't have: a drive that even his closest friends admired in him. Mauricio never stopped before an obstacle. He thought about it and kept thinking about it until the solution was clear in his mind. And then he acted upon it and worked on it until the problem was solved. At that point, he would normally move to another task and start the process again. But, like he had just said, he now had people helping him create what was inside his brain. It hadn't been always like that. When Guen, Arias, Leander, and Mauricio had first settled inside the rocky formation nestled between canyons, they'd had to fight every possible adversity by themselves. When they had started building the foundation of the city, they had been utterly alone, and more than once, despair had settled in their midst like an unwanted guest. But Mauricio had never complained in front of the others. He had shouldered the others' pain, given back solace and never asked for anything in return.

"Take the first drink of water." Leander was holding the tin bucket to Mauricio's mouth, full to the rim and sweating with cold dew.

"To everybody!" Mauricio raised the bucket, the men cheered loudly, and then he sipped the liquid carefully as if it was a precious wine. He closed his eyes and turned his face toward the darkening sky and thanked the Heavens.

"Let the celebration begin! Free day tomorrow for everybody!" the Priest decreed and the men went wild with happiness. Someone already had a guitar ready and spontaneous singing took place in a matter of minutes.

Later that night, Mauricio retreated into a corner away from the central plaza, happy to look at what they had accomplished as a community. The men were all there dancing and singing. The women were all staying in the same spot, still wary of being in the same place with so many ex-slaves, but nobody was bothering them. After a few hours, the bravest of them had decided to attempt some dancing in the central square where all the action was. Mauricio was even happier to see that a few of the families from the Caves had decided to join the festivities. He saw Lucas twirling around, giddy with the music and the colors.

"You wish she were here." Guen had approached silently, but Mauricio saw her coming and wasn't surprised by her presence.

"Always. There isn't a single moment I don't wish she were here," he answered, taking the hand she had gently put on his shoulder and kissing it affectionately.

"Have you received any new news about your daughter?" Guen asked, as she always did when they were alone.

Lately, the Priest always had an entourage of loyal men escorting him everywhere, hoping to learn from him everything he knew. Mauricio had been forced to reclaim some free time during his busy days to be able to relax. He loved his desert-sculpting time, because he decided who was allowed to follow him outside the city. Normally, he asked Lucas to accompany him to the desert, since the boy's home was on the way.

"I haven't. Only the same old things, and I'm not even sure that everything they write is true. It could be propaganda, but I like to read about her anyway. I wish I could see a picture of Maurice, but I understand that Rosie is protecting her as best as she can." Mauricio had his eyes on the central square, where a boy was flirting with a girl. Mauricio smiled and wondered how old the boy could be.

"I've always meant to ask you something…" Guen started, her eyes on the dancing couple as well.

"Shoot." Mauricio didn't know what she wanted to ask, but he knew it had everything to do with Rosie.

"Why have you never tried to contact her? Or at least let her know you're still alive?" Guen turned to look directly at him.

"I thought about it in the beginning. Then, when I was going to send her a message, the news of her marriage arrived and by the time I read it, she had already been married more than five months and the baby was due soon. I thought that she deserved a chance to be happy. The last time I saw her, she was upset because she already knew that we weren't going to see each other anymore. But she lied to me to make me feel better. Writing to her when she had already started a new life with her wife seemed a cruel thing to do." Mauricio smiled when the boy stole a small kiss from the girl.

"Do you regret your decision?" Guen hadn't turned around and her eyes were focused on him.

"No, I still love her. I hope that she found happiness with the girl she was forced to marry. Rosie told me that she knew who they had in mind, and that she was a good person." Mauricio was still following the boy's clumsy attempts at courting.

"But, aren't you jealous? I couldn't bear the idea of Arias married to someone else." Guen was trying to shake Mauricio from the torpor that seemed to have become his second skin lately. He had barely noticed before, but now he could see a pattern in his closest friends' behavior toward him. Lucas had been pestering him for weeks; Leander had been dancing a waltz around him as well; and now here was Guen and her inquisition. As he thought about it, even Arias had been strangely chatty, when he normally was rather taciturn.

"I try not to think about it, obviously. If I do, I feel the need to haul rocks and run from one end of the desert to the other. I am human, and I suffer at the thought like anybody else. But I had to give her at least a chance to be free of me. And maybe she managed to build a life with that girl, and they are happy together. Maurice doesn't know that she has a father; she is ten now and she has a normal life. She's a pure breed. Do you think I could live with myself if I destroyed her happiness with a truth that is almost impossible to prove? It would be my word against the mighty Priestess'. And as much as I'd like to free all the men in Ginecea, we're not organized enough to launch a full-scale war against the pure breeds. And in the end, I would be my daughter's worst enemy. I would be the one she would hate the most." Mauricio noticed how the girl was holding hands with the boy.

"But, you know the day will come when you have to decide," Guen said softly.

"And when we are strong enough to declare war on Ginecea, I'll decide without a second of hesitation. The City of Men is counting on me to do the right thing, and I won't disappoint those men and women. Not for my gain, not for my weakness. It will kill me, but I won't think twice about giving the orders." Mauricio's heart rejoiced at the sight of the young couple sitting on a bench talking to each other, oblivious that there was a world outside where they couldn't even exchange looks without being exiled from society.

"Look at them—" Mauricio pointed out the lovely scene unfolding before their eyes. "—they're not the only ones who'll grow old together like you and Arias. Lucas' family is not the only one living peacefully inside the Caves. Leander and Julius are an example for many who will adopt boys and girls without making any distinction between genders. This is what I want. One day, there will be another Mauricio and another Rosie, and they will be happy together. They will love and have quarrels. They'll have kids and maybe even grow apart by choice. But it will be their decision." Mauricio looked at Guen and saw that she had tears in her eyes.

"And you still go out every day to scan the desert looking for her." Guen smiled at her friend of so many years with a tenderness that touched Mauricio deeply.

"And I still wait for her. Even though I know she'll never appear at the horizon, I go out every day looking because doing so was the only thing that kept me sane when we first arrived here. Back then, when the time passed slowly and it was painfully obvious that she wasn't coming, I still drew strength from the act of waiting. I got used to it, and now it is part of my daily routine. Love is a powerful tool. It can elevate your mind to peaks you never before experienced. It can free your body from pain. I needed that then, and I need that now more than ever. Hoping, even foolishly, that one day I will see Rosie again keeps me going when I am tired." Mauricio wiped away Guen's tears with his fingers and kissed her head.

"I care for you. And it pains me to see you alone," Guen said, smiling at Mauricio.

"I care for you, too. Don't be sad for me. I didn't choose whom to love, but I wouldn't change it, either, if I could have. Ultimately, Rosie is the reason why we're all here. If she only knew what her love started…" Mauricio said and then laughed softly. "But, don't mind me. I don't want to ruin your night with my melancholy. On a night like this, when people poke me around, I tend to grow nostalgic."

"I think that on nights like this, you finally say what's in your heart."

"Still, I have no right to dump on everyone else's mood." Mauricio smiled at her and waved one hand in the air to dismiss the topic.

"Since you have declared tomorrow free, we're going to have Leander's family over for dinner. Would you like to join us, or do you see enough of your god-daughters at school that you don't wish to see them outside of it as well?" Guen knew that he couldn't refuse such an invitation and grinned at her friend in triumph.

"You were always good at guilt-tripping people when it's convenient for you," Mauricio complained, but nodded at the same time. "I'll be late though."

"I haven't told you the time, yet!" Guen laughed at his childish game of power.

"Regardless. I won't subject myself to your presence more than necessary," he joked and Guen punched him in the shoulder.

"Ouch! Is this the way to treat the Priest?" Mauricio asked while massaging the injured limb.

"Don't even get me started with that, *Your Holiness*." It was their private joke when nobody was listening.

"I feel that I never tell you enough, but, thank you, again. I'll be forever grateful for what you did back in Tarin. You risked your life for me; you were good to me and Rosie; you gave us precious moments together, and without your help, I wouldn't be here." Mauricio repeated words that he had already said many times. But tonight, it was different. The City of Men was at a turning point. After so many years of being constantly on the brink of extinction, it was finally facing the first big reprieve. It was the right time to acknowledge true friendships.

"I felt that you deserved a few good days, or at least as good as I could give you, given our circumstances." Guen shyly shrugged her shoulders.

"And to think that you despised Rosie so much." Mauricio almost laughed at remembering how Guen had acted when in her presence.

"I couldn't stand her and everything she represented, but when I discovered the sentiments she harbored for you, I understood that she was a different person altogether." Guen paused for a moment, and Mauricio had the impression that she was lost in her own memories of Rosie. "I'm glad I met the true Rosie—not the brat everybody thought her to be, not the spoiled first daughter who hid herself under a shallow mask. Just her, a selfless girl who helped you escape your fate. I liked that Rosie very much, and we would have been the greatest friends in Ginecea. I miss her too, you know?" she finished.

"Life would have been just perfect with her by my side," he said, looking at the young couple sneaking away around the corner.

CHAPTER 13

"Priest, how do you feel today?" Lucas was looking worriedly at Mauricio's wrinkled face.

"I admit that time hasn't been kind to me, but I am not one hundred, yet. Not even seventy. You shouldn't be so disrespectful to the Priest," Mauricio joked.

"I didn't mean to—"

"Just teasing you." Mauricio smiled at Lucas and then added, "Don't worry. I'm not going to die today. I still have several things to do before getting my well-deserved rest." He was cold, and he hadn't slept at all, but Lucas' affection was enough to make him lie about his condition.

"It's not funny. I keep telling you, but you simply don't listen." Lucas threw his hands in the air to communicate his despair, but only succeeded at being comedic. His face was wrinkled prematurely by the merciless sun of the desert and showed more than he wanted.

Mauricio laughed and his ribs ached. "When you reach my age, you don't care about listening so much anymore." Mauricio patted the couch and gestured for Lucas to join him there.

"Tell me about your son. How is Randal? I want to hear about *him*." Mauricio's voice wasn't faint, but he wasn't sure he had fooled Lucas.

"Randal thinks he's in love with a new boy now. If I remember correctly, this is a record even for him. He changes his heart once a month, but this new love replaced the other after just a week. I hope he'll settle one day for a good person and be happy with whomever he chooses." Lucas always complained about his son.

"He's a good boy. You worry too much. You'll see. When you're a grandfather, everything your son did wrong will magically disappear." Mauricio smiled.

"Which reminds me, I brought you the latest news from Ginecea." Lucas smiled back and went to retrieve a bundle of magazines he had put on the bookshelves at the entry of the Priest's apartment. "Here it is. There is something about your granddaughter—" He leafed through the magazines until he found what he was looking for. "—a new picture and a whole article about some summer camp Pax is going to attend while her mother is preparing her campaign." He gave the Priest the magazine and pointed at the picture of a slender girl with chestnut hair and big, hazel eyes. "She really is beautiful," Lucas commented proudly as if he were talking about his daughter. He knew more about the Priest's famous granddaughter than he knew about his other friends' kids.

"Yes, she is. And she is smart, too. You can see how clever she is from the bright light in her eyes. She'll do great things."

"It seems that your daughter has a very good chance of winning the election." Lucas had never lost the propensity to ask all the questions nobody had the brass to ask the Priest. But with age, he had learned how to temper his impulsive character. He had been dancing around the question for days, since he had known that Maurice was running for President of Ginecea. Now the unasked question was hanging between them, threatening to ruin their perfectly-oiled, morning routine.

"Go ahead. Ask what you want to ask." Mauricio had decided long ago that it was fun to play with Lucas, and now that the sources of his amusement were scarce, that was one of the few pleasures left to him.

"What kind of President do you think she would be?" Lucas asked.

"What can I say—" Mauricio opened and closed his hands to lessen the stiffness and let the blood circulate. "—I can only hope that she'll be more open-minded than the last three. Unfortunately, I don't have a magic ball, like some believe," Mauricio answered truthfully, adding a touch of dryness at the end. He had grown tired of the people who worshipped him and believed that he had an answer for everything. He was thankful for Lucas' friendship because the man allowed him to be himself: old and cranky.

"Things have been hard for the slaves lately," Lucas commented with an ironic understatement. The slaves' conditions had deteriorated since Maurice's grandmother's presidency. Rosie's mother had been at least fair for being a pure breed. Although she hadn't done anything to better the slaves' lives, she hadn't done anything to worsen them, either, which was more than could be said about the other three presidents Ginecea had elected since then. The Tarin incident and his escape became what the pure breeds needed to launch a full-scale repression of an already repressed and beaten population of men. It didn't matter it was a woman who actually committed the multiple murders and attempted to kill the President's daughter. The accident got an outrageous cover up, and now, every pure breed girl in Ginecea studied in school that men, soulless creatures with animalistic instincts, had taken the lives of valiant guards, who had children and families, that tragic night.

"I don't think that we're going to see big changes soon, anyway," Mauricio said cautiously. He owed Lucas some hope, but he didn't want to lead him around chasing wild dreams.

"You don't think that your daughter would be sympathetic to our cause?" Lucas asked, shifting around.

Mauricio kept silent for a long moment. He didn't want to consider the possibility that his own daughter could be the next bad president—the next butcher, as her predecessors had been called by the male population, and for good reason. Thousands of innocent slaves had died victims of poor hygienic conditions, starvation, and, most of all, indifference. The City of Men had mourned their friends and relatives with a monthly ceremony to commit the names of the fallen to memory. The Priest's sculpture garden had spontaneously become a memorial for the victims. Every month, rock by rock, a new sculpture was erected with the exact amount of stones as the number of men, and the occasional fathered woman, who had lost their lives.

"Honestly, I don't think she can even consider such a thought. To be sympathetic with our cause, you must at least acknowledge that slavery is a problem. Maurice has lived all her life as the purest of the pure breeds; for her, slavery is a part of society. Like the sun and the moon rotating between day and night. She could be a magnanimous president. But that, I am afraid, is the whole extent our hopes can travel." Mauricio felt exhausted.

"But what if she comes to know the truth about her birth?" Lucas was one of the few persons that knew about the relationship between the Priest and Maurice Layan. The others were Leander and Julius. Guen and Arias had been killed a few years before in a riot that had claimed several other lives; they died to defend the women's rights to live in the City of Men. Unfortunately, one of the side effects generated by the pure breeds' carnage of slaves had been a resurgence of hatred against women in the City of Men. Mauricio felt responsible for the massacre, and his health had started declining since then and never got better. He had never forgiven himself for the death of his closest friends, and eventually, the guilt dug a hole too deep into his heart. Now, in the box of memories that he kept under his bed, Mauricio also had a few mementos that belonged to Guen and Arias. Cordelia had been nice enough to give him something.

"She'd never believe me. The new Priestess would assure her about the holiness of the incognito. At the same time, the Priestess would be tipped off that we know and retaliate immediately against the slaves. We wouldn't stand a chance against an army of vengeful pure breeds." Mauricio had plenty of time to think nowadays. His health had declined to the point that he could barely leave his room. He was still leading the City of Men from his bed, and in the rare occasions he had slept the night before, he would lead the city from his couch. Since he didn't have to supervise the fields anymore, he could think, undisturbed, for hours. Sometimes he wished to be relieved from thinking, too. But his mind was still sharp and lying around in his apartment bored him greatly.

"But if we could find a way to prove it?" Lucas asked.

"You're late for patrol duty," Mauricio answered instead.

"Don't change the topic; it's not like we're going to talk about it later. So, what if we can prove it?"

"How? I thought about it for several years, but all the plans I made were flawed. We don't have either the power or the influence. We need the women's cooperation to succeed." Mauricio started his routine of stretching to reactivate the muscles in his sleepy legs.

"There are women who want to help us." Lucas pointed a finger outside the window to show the Priest the workers painting the internal walls of the city.

"Yes, but they're all fathered, and they barely have political rights." Mauricio took a look at the women working just outside his window. He waved one hand and they answered back immediately, calling his name.

"They can vote!" Lucas said with emphasis.

"Yes, but they have to elect one voter, who in turn is going to represent thousands of them. Their vote is hardly significant to further our cause." Mauricio, in the capacity of the Priest, greeted the women with gentle words of appreciation for their work.

"I understand that, but if they all decided to vote differently from what's suggested by their employers, their vote would start counting." Lucas was stubborn, and he knew he was on to something.

"In that case, yes, it would definitely change the balance. And if all the fathered women would rebel against the pure breeds, things could finally change in Ginecea." Mauricio blew a soft kiss with his hand toward a young girl who was smiling at him with affection.

"Hi, Lara. How is your mom?" the Priest asked the girl.

"Better. Thank you, sir, for sending the extra food for her," Lara answered with another big smile.

"Let me know if you need anything else." The Priest waved his hand at Lara, who bobbed her head, thanked him once more and then disappeared behind the open window to paint another part of the wall.

"Did you send them your dinner?" Lucas asked with a suspicious tone after the girl was out of sight.

"I wasn't hungry yesterday, and I hate wasting food. You know I can't stand the idea." Mauricio had hoped that Lucas wouldn't discover his little deceptions. It wasn't the first time, but he had managed, until now, to hide it successfully.

"I'll tell Lorena that you don't like her food," Lucas said with a mock hurt tone for the alleged slight toward his sister's culinary skills.

"Good try. Lorena knows I only eat what she cooks." Mauricio liked the fact that they could still laugh and joke, even after so many years of knowing each other.

"Anyway, coming back to whatever we were talking about before you tried to entertain the girls with your charm…" Lucas started, but Mauricio stopped him.

"The fathered women would never rebel against the pure breeds. Although they should, for the way they're treated." His eyes went to the window again to look for the sky looming brightly through the enormous skylight that illuminated the inside of the city.

"But—" Lucas couldn't let it go.

"They would lose what little they have to help the men. They resent the pure breeds because they want to be like them. Siding with the slaves is not going to be on their agenda for a long time, unless something happens to make them change their minds." Mauricio closed his eyes and basked in the sun.

"Well, we'll have to work on that, then." Lucas stood up.

"Have a safe patrol today, and let's hope that you can save some lives," Mauricio offered his usual blessing and accepted Lucas' tender hug.

"I will bring you some fresh recruits. I have a good feeling this morning." Lucas smiled and turned around.

Mauricio watched the man until the door closed behind him and then went to retrieve his box from under his bed. He opened it reverentially, as usual, and took out the only picture he had left of Rosie. It was a clipping from the day of her marriage, and she looked exactly like the last time he had seen her. She was lovely in her wedding gown and she was looking straight ahead of her—as if she was looking at him.

"I'll see you soon, my love." He stroked the fading image on the much-abused piece of paper. "We'll meet in a place where nobody will tear us apart."

BACKSTORY AND ACKNOWLEDGMENTS

While I was writing *Pax in the Land of Women*, two characters, Rosie and the Priest, came to life. I thought that their story deserved to be told, but *Pax* was already on its way to completion, and there wasn't any space left in it for them. 2010 Nanowrimo came along, and I jumped at the opportunity to write 50,000 words around the slave and the President's daughter. Last November, while my DH was playing Red Dead Redemption, I sat by him on the couch and wrote *The Priest*. And that is the reason why every time I think about this novel I automatically hear RDR's soundtrack in my mind.

I feel I have several people to thank. I'll start with my parents, from whom I have inherited a passion for reading. I'll never thank my father enough for giving me a copy of *I, Robot* when I was seven years old. I owe many thanks to my friend, and loyal beta reader, Claudia, who has been patient enough to follow my journey through almost every word I have written. My everlasting gratitude goes to Alessandro for creating the cover. My love goes to my kids just for being them. Finally, without my husband's support, none of this would be possible. The biggest thanks of all is to Roberto, who never complains about the ruin that has become our house, and who has read my stories, even though they aren't his cup of tea.

PERSONS OF INTEREST

A book is never a solitary endeavor, although the writer oftentimes thinks otherwise.

Amy Eye edited *The Priest*.
Cassie McCown proofread it.
Roberto Ruggeri formatted the novel.
Alessandro Fiorini created the cover.
You, hopefully, read the book.

BIO

Monica La Porta is an Italian who landed in Seattle several years ago. Despite popular feelings about the Northwest weather, she finds the mist and the rain the perfect conditions to write. Being a strong advocate of universal acceptance and against violence in any form and shape, she is also glad to have landed precisely in Washington State. She is the author of The Ginecean Chronicles, a dystopian/science fiction series set on the planet Ginecea where women rule over a race of enslaved men and heterosexual love is considered a sin. She has published *The Priest, Pax in the Land of Women*, and *Prince at War*. She is currently editing the fourth in the Ginecean series. She also wrote and illustrated a children's book about the power of imagination, *The Prince's Day Out*. Her latest published short, *Linda of the Night*, is a fairytale love story celebrating inner beauty. Stop by her blog to read about her miniatures, sculptures, paintings, and her beloved beagle, Nero. Sometimes, she also posts about her writing.

Monica La Porta's blog:
http://www.monicalaporta.com

The Ginecean Chronicles on Facebook:
http://www.facebook.com/ginecea

The Prince's Day Out on Facebook:
http://www.facebook.com/ThePrincesDayOut

Monica's Author page on Goodreads:
http://www.goodreads.com/author/show/5757332.Monica_La_Por
ta

Monica on Twitter:
http://twitter.com/momilp

www.ingramcontent.com/pod-product-compliance
Lightning Source LLC
Chambersburg PA
CBHW071915220626
47052CB00002B/360